双语名著无障碍阅读丛书

鲁宾逊漂流记

Robinson Crusoe

[英国] 丹尼尔·笛福 著
高诚 译

中国出版集团
中译出版社

图书在版编目（CIP）数据

鲁宾逊漂流记：汉英对照/（英）笛福（Defoe，D.）著；高诚译. —北京：中译出版社，2012.7（2022.5重印）
（双语名著无障碍阅读丛书）
ISBN 978- 7- 5001- 3435- 0

I. ①鲁… II. ①笛… ②高… III. ①英语—汉语—对照读物 ②长篇小说—英国—现代 IV. ①H319.4：I

中国版本图书馆CIP数据核字（2012）第149781号

出版发行 / 中译出版社
地　　址 / 北京市西城区车公庄大街甲4号物华大厦六层
电　　话 /（010）68359827，68359303（发行部）；68359725（编辑部）
邮　　编 / 100044
传　　真 /（010）68357870
电子邮箱 / book@ctph.com.cn
网　　址 / http://www.ctph.com.cn

责任编辑 / 范祥镇
封面设计 / 潘　峰

排　　版 / 陈　彬

经　　销 / 新华书店

规　　格 / 710毫米×1000毫米　1/16
印　　张 / 9
字　　数 / 115千字
版　　次 / 2012年7月第一版
印　　次 / 2022年5月第十一次

ISBN 978-7-5001-3435-0　　**定价**：18. 00元

出版前言

多年以来，中译出版社有限公司（原中国对外翻译出版有限公司）凭借国内一流的翻译和出版实力及资源，精心策划、出版了大批双语读物，在海内外读者中和业界内产生了良好、深远的影响，形成了自己鲜明的出版特色。

二十世纪八九十年代出版的英汉（汉英）对照“一百丛书”，声名远扬，成为一套最权威、最有特色且又实用的双语读物，影响了一代又一代英语学习者和中华传统文化研究者、爱好者；还有“英若诚名剧译丛”、“中华传统文化精粹丛书”、“美丽英文书系”，这些优秀的双语读物，有的畅销，有的常销不衰反复再版，有的被选为大学英语阅读教材，受到广大读者的喜爱，获得了良好的社会效益和经济效益。

“双语名著无障碍阅读丛书”是中译专门为中学生和英语学习者精心打造的又一品牌，是一个新的双语读物系列，具有以下特点：

选题创新——该系列图书是国内第一套为中小学生量身打造的双语名著读物，所选篇目均为教育部颁布的语文新课标必读书目，或为中学生以及同等文化水平的社会读者喜闻乐见的世界名著，重新编译为英汉（汉英）对照的双语读本。这些书既给青少年读者提供了成长过程中不可或缺的精神食粮，又让他们领略到原著的精髓和魅力，对他们更好地学习英文大有裨益；同时，丛书中入选的《论语》、《茶馆》、《家》等汉英对照读物，亦是热爱中国传统文化的中外读者所共知的经典名篇，能使读者充分享受阅读经典的无限乐趣。

无障碍阅读——中学生阅读世界文学名著的原著会遇到很多生词和文化难点。针对这一情况，我们给每一本读物原文中的较难词汇和不易理解之处都加上了注释，在内文的版式设计上也采取英汉（或汉英）对照方式，扫清了学生阅读时的障碍。

优良品质——中译双语读物多年来在读者中享有良好口碑，这得益于作者和出版者对于图书质量的不懈追求。“双语名著无障碍阅读丛书”继承了中译双语读物的优良传统——精选的篇目、优秀的译文、方便实用的注解，秉承着对每一个读者负责的精神，竭力打造精品图书。

愿这套丛书成为广大读者的良师益友，愿读者在英语学习和传统文化学习两方面都取得新的突破。

Daniel Defoe

ROBINSON CRUSOE

My mother's relations were named Robinson, a very good family in that country, and from whom I was called Robinson Kreutznaer; but, by the usual corruption of words in England, we are now called—nay we call ourselves and write our name—Crusoe; and so my companions always called me.

My head began to be filled very early with **rambling**① thoughts. My father, who was very ancient, had given me a **competent**② share of learning, as far as house-education and a country free school generally go.

He designed me for the law. But I would be satisfied with nothing but going to sea.

My **inclination**③ to this led me so strongly against the will, nay, the commands of my father, and against all the **entreaties**④ and persuasions of my mother and other friends, that there seemed to be something **fatal**⑤ in that **propensity**⑥ of nature, tending directly to the life of misery which was to **befall**⑦ me.

My father, a wise and grave man, gave me serious and excellent counsel against what he **foresaw**⑧ was my design.

鲁宾逊漂流记

我母亲娘家姓鲁宾逊，是当地一个很体面的人家。由于这个缘故，我就叫上了鲁宾逊·克鲁兹那这个名字。但由于英国语音的变化，现在无论人们叫我们、我们称呼或写自己姓名都成了“克鲁索”，因此我的朋友也就这样称呼我了。

我从小脑子里就有云游四海的念头。我那年迈的老父亲让我接受了相当程度的教育，除了家庭教育之外，还让我接受了乡村义务教育。

他的本意是让我学习法律，但我对什么都不感兴趣，一心一意想到海外去。

我这种强烈的信念，使我对于老父亲的意愿和他的命令持强烈的反对态度，而且对于母亲的恳求和我的朋友们的劝告也都一概予以拒绝。我这种顽固不化的怪脾气，似乎使我命中注定今后要遭遇种种不幸。

我父亲是一个精明而严肃的人，预见到了我的计划的危险性，向我提出了严肃而精辟的忠

① ramble /'ræmbl/ *v.* 漫步，漫游

② competent /'kɔmpitənt/ *a.* 足够的

③ inclination /ˌinkli'neiʃən/ *n.* 倾向，意愿

④ entreaty /in'triːti/ *n.* 恳求，哀求

⑤ fatal /'feitl/ *a.* 致命的，毁灭性的

⑥ propensity /prə'pensiti/ *n.* 倾向，习性

⑦ befall /bi'fɔːl/ *v.* 降临

⑧ foresee /fɔː'siː/ *v.* 预见，预知

He called me one morning into his chamber, where he was **confined**① by the **gout**②, and **expostulated**③ very warmly with me upon this subject. He asked me what reasons, more than a mere wandering inclination, I had for leaving father's house and my native country, where I might be well introduced, and had a **prospect**④ of raising my fortune by **application**⑤ and **industry**⑥, with a life of **ease**⑦ and pleasure.

He told me it was men of desperate fortunes on one hand, or of **aspiring**⑧, superior fortunes on the other, who went abroad upon adventures, to rise by **enterprise**⑨, and make themselves famous in undertakings of a nature out of the common road; that these things were all either too far above me or too far below me; that mine was the middle state, or what might be called the upper station of low life, which he had found, by long experience, was the best state in the world, the most suited to human happiness, not exposed to the miseries and hardships, the labour and sufferings of the **mechanic**⑩ part of mankind, and not embarrassed with the pride, luxury, ambition, and envy of the upper part of mankind. He told me I might judge of the happiness of this state by this one thing—viz. that this was the state of life which all other people envied; that kings have frequently **lamented**⑪ the miserable consequence of being born to great things, and wished they had been placed in the middle of the two extremes, between the mean and the great.

After this he pressed me **earnestly**⑫, and in the most **affectionate**⑬ manner, not to play the young man, nor to **precipitate**⑭ myself into miseries which nature, and the station of life I was born in, seemed to have provided against; that I was under no necessity of seeking my

告。

一天早晨，他把我叫到他的房间，他因为害痛风病不能走动，就此语重心常地规劝了一番。他问我，除仅仅为了到外面瞎跑以外，我有什么理由要离开自己的父母和家乡？他说，我在这里可以仰仗亲友们的推荐，还有自己的勤勉，会有一份很不错的家业，过一辈子舒坦快乐的生活。

他告诉我，那些到海外去闯荡冒险、去开创事业，甚至希望通过非常规的方式使自己扬名后世的人，不外乎是两种人：一种是穷困潦倒、急于发财的人；另一种是野心勃勃、富于资财的人。但是这两种情况对我来说，不是太高就是太低，而我正处于这两者之间，或者可以称之为中间阶层。凭他多年的体会，他认为这是世上最好的阶层，最适合于给人以幸福的阶层，既不必像那些体力劳动者那样使自己艰苦劳作而备受各种痛苦和折磨，也不必像那些上层人物为骄奢、尔虞我诈所烦恼。他告诉我，我可以用一件事来判断这种生活地位是否幸福，那就是，是否其他所有人都羡慕这种生活方式。许多帝王常常感叹由于他们高贵的出身而导致的不幸后果，梦想自己能够被置于两个极端的中间，也就是位于贵贱两者之间。

说完这些，他极其诚恳地劝我不要耍小孩子脾气，不要无端自寻烦恼，因为就我的本性和我出生的家庭生活状况而言，这些都是可以避免的。就我的家境来说，我没有必要出去找饭吃，

①confine /kən'fain/ *v.* 限制，闭居

② gout /gɑut/ *n.* 痛风

③ expostulate /iks'pɔstjuleit/ *v.* （对人或行为的）告诫

④ prospect /'prɔspekt/ *n.* 希望，展望

⑤ application /ˌæpli'keiʃən/ *n.* 勤勉，专心

⑥ industry /'indəstri/ *n.* 勤勉，刻苦

⑦ ease /iːz/ *n.* 安逸，悠闲

⑧ aspire /ə'spaiə/ *v.* 热望，立志

⑨ enterprise /'entəpraiz/ *n.* （冒险性的）计划

⑩ mechanic /mi'kænik/ *a.* 手工的，体力的

⑪ lament /lə'ment/ *v.* 哀悼，悔恨

⑫ earnestly /'əːnistli/ *ad.* 认真地，真切地

⑬ affectionate /ə'fekʃənit/ *a.* 情深的，充满情爱的

⑭ precipitate /pri'sipiteit/ *v.* 使……陷入

bread; that he would do well for me, and **endeavour**① to enter me fairly into the station of life which he had just been recommending to me; in a word, that as he would do very kind things for me if I would stay and settle at home as he directed, so he would not have so much hand in my misfortunes as to give me any encouragement to go away; and to close all, he told me I had my elder brother for an example, to whom he had used the same earnest persuasions to keep him from going into the Low Country wars, but could not **prevail**②, his young desires **prompting**③ him to run into the army, where he was killed.

Tears ran down his face very plentifully, especially when he spoke of my brother who was killed; and that when he spoke of my having **leisure**④ to **repent**⑤, and none to assist me, he was so moved that he broke off the **discourse**⑥, and told me his heart was so full he could say no more to me.

I was sincerely affected with this discourse, and, indeed, who could be otherwise? And I **resolved**⑦ not to think of going abroad any more, but to settle at home according to my father's desire. But alas! A few days wore it all off; and, in short, to prevent any of my father's further **importunities**⑧, in a few weeks after I resolved to run quite away from him. However, I did not act quite so **hastily**⑨ as the first heat of my resolution prompted; but I took my mother at a time when I thought her a little more pleasant than ordinary, and told her that my thoughts were so entirely bent upon seeing the world that I should never settle to anything with resolution enough to go through with it, and my father had better give me his **consent**⑩ than force me to go without it.

This put my mother into a great passion; she told me she knew it

他会为我做好一切，而且他要尽力帮助我过上他刚才向我大力推荐的那种好生活。简而言之，他说只要我照着他说的做，好好待在家里，他一定会为我安排好一切；因此，他不会对我的远游给予任何鼓励，免得对我的不幸承担责任。最后作为结束语，他又让我以我哥哥为前车之鉴。他曾经同样认真地劝说我哥哥，叫他不要去佛兰德打仗，但他就是不听，凭着一股青年人的热情参了军，结果却在那里送了命。

只见他一边说一边老泪纵横，特别是提到我那死去的哥哥的时候。当他讲到我将来闲下来肯定会后悔，而且到那时无人能帮、孤立无援，竟然哽咽得说不下去了。他说他太伤感了，没法对我说什么了。

我被父亲的话深深地感动了，真的，在那种场合谁能不被感染呢？我下决心打消出去的念头，听父亲的话，好好待在家里。唉，没过几天，我就把它忘了个干干净净。简单说来，为了避免父亲总在我耳边唠唠叨叨，几个星期以后，我决定逃得远远的。然而，我没有像第一次下决心那样急于行动。我必须等我母亲，等到我认为她比往常高兴的时候，再向她提出我的想法。告诉她我非常想去外面开开眼界，告诉她由于这个信仰始终缠着我，使我在这里无法静下心来做任何事，我父亲不如痛痛快快地答应我，不要逼我逃离这个家庭。

我的这番话让母亲极为恼怒。她告诉我，她

① endeavour /in'devə/ *v.* 努力，尽力

② prevail /pri'veil/ *v.* 获胜

③ prompt /prɔmpt/ *v.* 激起，推动

④ leisure /'leʒə/ *n.* 空闲，闲暇

⑤ repent /ri'pent/ *v.* 后悔，悔悟

⑥ discourse /dis'kɔːs/ *n.* 讲话，演说

⑦ resolve /ri'zɔlv/ *v.* 决定，决心

⑧ importunity /ˌimpɔː'tjuːnəti/ *n.* 硬要，强求

⑨ hastily /'heistili/ *ad.* 匆忙地，急速地

⑩ consent /kən'sent/ *n.* 同意，许可

would be to no purpose to speak to my father upon any such subject; that he knew too well what was my interest to give his consent to anything so much for my hurt; and that she wondered how I could think of any such thing after the discourse I had had with my father, and such kind and **tender**① expressions as she knew my father had used to me; and that, in short, if I would **ruin**② myself, there was no help for me; but I might depend I should never have their consent to it; that for her part she would not have so much hand in my destruction; and I should never have it to say that my mother was willing when my father was not.

Though my mother refused to move it to my father, yet I heard afterwards that she reported all the discourse to him, and that my father, after showing a great concern at it, said to her, with a sigh, "That boy might be happy if he would stay at home; but if he goes abroad, he will be the most miserable **wretch**③ that ever was born; I can give no consent to it."

It was not till almost a year after this that I broke loose, though, in the meantime, I continued **obstinately**④ deaf to all proposals of settling to business, and frequently expostulated with my father and mother about their being so positively determined against what they knew my inclinations prompted me to. But being one day at Hull, where I went casually, and without any purpose of making an **elopement**⑤ at that time; but, I say, being there, and one of my companions being about to sail to London in his father's ship, and prompting me to go with them with the common **allurement**⑥ of **seafaring**⑦ men, that it should cost me nothing for my passage, I consulted neither father nor mother any more, nor so much as sent them word of it; but leaving them to

知道跟我父亲谈论这类话题根本没有用，因为他太清楚这种利害关系了，绝对不会答应这种对我有害的事情。她觉得奇怪的是，在我与父亲经过那次谈话以后，她知道他给了我谆谆告诫，我怎么还会想到这类事情。总之，她说如果我要自寻绝路，谁也不会帮助我，更不用说指望得到他们的同意。至于她自己，她绝不会帮助我自取灭亡，这样我以后永远也没有理由说，当时我父亲反对我这样做，而我母亲却同意。

尽管我母亲不肯把我的想法告诉我父亲，但我后来却听说，她把我们的谈话全盘告诉了我父亲。我父亲听后非常忧虑，对她叹息道："这孩子如果待在家里肯定很幸福，但是，如果他要漂泊在外，一定是世界上最苦命的人。我不能答应他。"

就在这事发生不到一年的时候，我憋不住了。在此期间，我对我父母亲要我干点正事的建议充耳不闻，经常与他们争吵，抱怨他们既然知道了我心里的想法还那么粗暴地干涉我。然而有一天，我恰巧到赫尔城去，在去的时候我还没有任何逃跑的打算。可是我得说，当我到了那里之后，我的一位朋友正打算坐他父亲的船到伦敦去，他用通常招收水手的方式，怂恿我跟他一块去，那也就是说让我免费旅行。于是，我既没有去征得父母亲的同意，也没有给他们捎去只言片语，就让他们自己随便去打听好了，只有上帝知

① tender /ˈtendə/ *a.* 温和的，亲切的

② ruin /ruin/ *v.* 毁坏，破坏

③ wretch /retʃ/ *n.* 可怜的人，家伙

④ obstinately /ˈɔbstinitli/ *ad.* 固执地，顽固地

⑤ elopement /iˈləupmənt/ *n.* 潜逃，私奔

⑥ allurement /əˈljuəmənt/ *n.* 引诱，诱惑

⑦ seafaring /ˈsiːfeəriŋ/ *a.* 航海的，跟航海有关的

hear of it as they might, without asking God's blessing or my father's, without any consideration of circumstances or consequences, and in an ill hour, God knows, on the 1st of September 1651, I went on board a ship **bound for**[1] London.

The ship was no sooner out of the Humber than the wind began to blow and the sea to rise in a most frightful manner; and, as I had never been at sea before, I was most inexpressibly sick in body and terrified in mind. I began now seriously to reflect upon what I had done, and how justly I was **overtaken**[2] by the judgment of Heaven for my **wicked**[3] leaving my father's house, and **abandoning**[4] my duty. All the good counsels of my parents, my father's tears and my mother's entreaties, came now fresh into my mind; and my **conscience**[5], which was not yet come to the **pitch**[6] of hardness to which it has since, **reproached**[7] me with the **contempt**[8] of advice, and the **breach**[9] of my duty to God and my father.

These wise and **sober**[10] thoughts continued all the while the storm lasted, and indeed some time after; but the next day the wind was **abated**[11], and the sea calmer, and I began to be a little **inured**[12] to it.

In a word, as the sea was returned to its smoothness of surface and settled calmness by the abatement of that storm, so the hurry of my thoughts being over, my fears and apprehensions of being **swallowed**[13] up by the sea being forgotten, and the **current**[14] of my former desires returned, I entirely forgot the vows and promises that I made in my **distress**[15].

It was my **lot**[16] first of all to fall into pretty good company in London. I first **got acquainted with**[17] the master of a ship who had been on the coast of Guinea; and who, having had very good success there,

道，我既没祈求上帝的祝福或我父亲的祝福，也没有考虑一下当时的处境和后果，就在1651年9月1日那个不祥的日子我登上了开往伦敦的船。

那只船刚刚走出亨伯河口就遇到了可怕的风浪，而且风力越来越大，十分可怕。我过去从来没有坐过船，因此感到全身有一种说不出来的难受，心里十分恐惧。我开始认真地想起我的所做所为，因为我私自离家出走，放弃了自己应尽的责任，上天对我的惩罚该有多么公平。所有我双亲善意的规劝，父亲的眼泪，母亲的恳求，一切一切都重新涌上我的心头。我的良心当时还没有像后来那样到了不可救药的地步，受到了谴责，因为我藐视别人的忠告，放弃了对上帝和父亲的责任。

这些明智而清醒的想法，从暴风雨发作到停息以后的一段时间里，一直盘据着我的脑海；但是到了第二天，风息浪止，我也有些开始习惯了。

总的来说，当风暴渐渐平息下去的时候，大海又安静下来，海面风平浪静，我那慌乱的情绪也平定了，我忘记了担心被海浪吞没的恐惧与忧虑，过去的想法又像潮水一样涌上了心头。我完全忘记了我在危难之中发出的誓言。

这是我所有冒险中的第一次，总算幸运，我在伦敦居然碰到了好人。我一开始就结识了一位到过几内亚的船主，他在那边生意做得不错，所以决定再去冒险。他对我的谈话非常感兴趣，也

① bound for 准备去，开往……的

② overtake /'əuvə'teik/ *v.* 赶上，突然来袭

③ wicked /'wikid/ *a.* 坏的，邪恶的

④ abandon /ə'bændən/ *v.* 放弃，遗弃

⑤ conscience /'kɔnʃəns/ *n.* 良心

⑥ pitch /pitʃ/ *n.* 程度

⑦ reproach /ri'prəutʃ/ *v.* 责备，申斥

⑧ contempt /kən'tempt/ *n.* 轻视，轻蔑

⑨ breach /briːtʃ/ *n.* 违背

⑩ sober /'səubə/ *a.* 清醒的，稳重的

⑪ abate /ə'beit/ *v.* 缓和，减弱

⑫ inure /i'njuə/ *v.* 使……习惯

⑬ swallow /'swɔləu/ *v.* 吞下，咽下

⑭ current /'kʌrənt/ *n.* 思潮，潮流

⑮ distress /dis'tres/ *n.* 苦恼

⑯ lot /lɔt/ *n.* 运气，命运

⑰ get acquainted with 知悉，了解

was resolved to go again. This captain taking a fancy to my conversation, which was not at all disagreeable at that time, hearing me say I had a mind to see the world, told me if I would go the voyage with him I should be at no expense; I should be his **messmate**① and his companion; and if I could carry anything with me, I should have all the advantage of it that the trade would admit; and perhaps I might meet with some encouragement.

I embraced the offer; and entering into a strict friendship with this captain.

Under him also I got a competent knowledge of the mathematics and the rules of **navigation**②, learned how to keep an account of the ship's course, take an observation, and, in short, to understand some things that were needful to be understood by a sailor; for, as he took delight to instruct me, I took delight to learn; and, in a word, this voyage made me both a sailor and a merchant.

I was now set up for a Guinea trader; and my friend, to my great misfortune, dying soon after his arrival, I resolved to go the same voyage again, and I **embarked**③ in the same vessel with one who was his mate in the former voyage, and had now got the command of the ship.

This was the unhappiest voyage that ever man made.

It was surprised in the grey of the morning by a Turkish **rover**④ of Sallee, who gave **chase**⑤ to us with all the sail she could make.

We **plied**⑥ them with small shot, half-pikes, powder-chests, and such like, and cleared our deck of them twice. However, to cut short this **melancholy**⑦ part of our story, our ship being disabled, and three of our men killed, and eight wounded, we were obliged to **yield**⑧, and

许那时因为我的谈话还不太让人讨厌。他听我说想去海外见识见识，便对我说，如果我同他一起去，我不必花什么钱，可以和他一起吃饭，就算他的伙计。他告诉我，如果我能随身带点货，他能给我提供诸多便利条件，让我做生意，也许我还可以赚点钱回来。

① messmate /ˈmesmeit/ *n.* 同餐之友，同餐桌的伙伴

我立刻接受了他的邀请，并且与这位船主成了亲密的朋友。

在他的指导下，我也学会了足够的数学知识，同时我还掌握了航海规程，学会了如何记录船只的航程，怎样观测天文。总而言之，我懂得了一个船员应该懂得的一些知识。船主很乐意教我，我也很乐意学。一句话，这次航行使我既成了一名船员，又成了一个商人。

② navigation /ˌnæviˈgeiʃən/ *n.* 航行，航海

我现在勉强算是一个几内亚商人，但十分不幸的是，我那朋友回国之后不久就死了。我决定再沿这条航线走一次，我和一个人一同登上了上次那条船，他原来是船上的大副，现在则成为船主了。

③ embark /imˈbaːk/ *v.* 乘船

这次航行是有史以来最为悲惨的航行。

有一天早晨，天刚刚亮，突然有一只从萨利来的土耳其海盗船，扯满了帆，从我们后面追了过来。

④ rover /ˈrəuvə/ *n.* 海盗（船）

⑤ chase /tʃeis/ *n.* 追捕，追逐

⑥ ply /plai/ *v.* 不断劝人吃喝，缠扰

我们用枪弹、刺刀、火药以及其他武器进行反击，打退了他们的两次进攻。但是，我不忍心再细说这段可悲的经过，最后我们的船只完全丧失了战斗能力，我们死了 3 个人，伤了 8 个，只

⑦ melancholy /ˈmelənkəli/ *a.* 忧沉的，使人悲伤的

⑧ yield /jiːld/ *v.* 屈服，投降

were carried all prisoners into Sallee, a port belonging to the Moors.

The usage I had there was not so **dreadful** [①] as at first I apprehended; nor was I carried up the country to the emperor's court, as the rest of our men were, but was kept by the captain of the rover as his proper prize, and made his slave, being young and **nimble**[②], and fit for his business.

Here I **meditated** [③] nothing but my escape, and what method I might take to effect it, but found no way that had the least probability in it.

After about two years, an **odd** [④] circumstance presented itself, which put the old thought of making some attempt for my liberty again in my head.

We went frequently out with a boat a-fishing; and as I was most **dexterous**[⑤] to catch fish for him, my **patron**[⑥] never went without me. It happened that he had appointed to go out in this boat, either for pleasure or for fish, with two or three Moors of some **distinction**[⑦] in that place, and for whom he had provided extraordinarily.

When by and by my patron came on board alone, and told me his guests had put off going from some business that fell out, and ordered me, with the man and boy, as usual, to go out with the boat and catch them some fish, for that his friends were to **sup**[⑧] at his house, and commanded that as soon as I got some fish I should bring it home to his house; all which I prepared to do.

This moment my former notions of **deliverance**[⑨] **darted**[⑩] into my thoughts, for now I found I was likely to have a little ship at my command.

After we had fished some time and caught nothing—for when I had

好被迫投降。我们被全部带到了萨利，那是一个摩尔人的港口。

我在那里的待遇并没有我所预料的那么可怕，但也并没有像其他人一样被带进皇宫，而是被留在海盗船船长家里，成了他的战利品，做了他的奴仆，因为我年轻伶俐，能满足他的需要。

在那里，我整天什么也不想，光琢磨着怎么逃走，以及采取什么方法才能逃走，但希望极为渺茫。

大约过了两年，我的处境发生了特殊变化，这使得争取自由的想法再次浮现在我的头脑中。

我们经常坐一只小艇外出打鱼，因为我最擅长给他捕鱼，我的主人每次都带我去。有一次，他与人相约乘这条船出去，既为休闲娱乐也为捕鱼，他约的人大约有两三个，都是当地有身份和地位的摩尔人，并为此做了充分准备。

不曾想到了后来，只有我的主人独自来到船上，告诉我他的客人临时有事取消外出，命令我同一个摩尔人和一个小孩子像往常一样出去替他打点鱼来，因为他的朋友当晚要来他家与他共进晚餐。他吩咐我，一旦打到鱼，我必须马上把鱼拿回家并送到他的房间。这些事我都准备一一照办。

这时候，先前争取自由的念头，又突然浮在了我的脑海中，因为我觉得现在已经有一只小船可供我支配了。

我们打了一会儿鱼，什么也没有打到，因为每逢有鱼上钩，我总把它们放掉，不让那个摩尔

① dreadful /ˈdredful/ *a.* 可怕的

② nimble /ˈnimbl/ *a.* 敏捷的，伶俐的

③ meditate /ˈmediteit/ *v.* 想，考虑

④ odd /ɔd/ *a.* 奇特的，古怪的

⑤ dexterous /ˈdekstərəs/ *a.* 灵巧的

⑥ patron /ˈpeitrən/ *n.* 恩主

⑦ distinction /disˈtiŋkʃən/ *n.* 优越，盛名

⑧ sup /sʌp/ *v.* 啜，尝

⑨ deliverance /diˈlivərəns/ *n.* 救出，释放

⑩ dart /daːt/ *v.* 投射，突进

fish on my hook I would not pull them up, that he might not see them—I said to the Moor, "This will not do; our master will not be thus served; we must stand farther off." He, thinking no harm, agreed, and being in the head of the boat, set the sails; and, as I had the **helm**①, I ran the boat out near a league farther, and then brought her to, as if I would fish; when, giving the boy the helm, I stepped forward to where the Moor was, and making as if I **stooped**② for something behind him, I took him by surprise with my arm under his waist, and **tossed**③ him clear overboard into the sea.

I could have been content to have taken this Moor with me, and have drowned the boy, but there was no **venturing**④ to trust him.

The boy smiled in my face, and spoke so innocently that I could not distrust him, and swore to be faithful to me, and go all over the world with me.

Yet such was the fright I had taken of the Moors, and the dreadful apprehensions I had of falling into their hands, that I would not stop, or go on shore, or come to an **anchor**⑤; the wind continuing fair till I had sailed in that manner five days; and then the wind shifting to the southward, I concluded also that if any of our vessels were in chase of me, they also would now give over; so I ventured to make to the coast, and came to an anchor in the mouth of a little river.

But as soon as it was quite dark, we heard such dreadful noises of the **barking**⑥, **roaring**⑦, and **howling**⑧ of wild creatures, of we knew not what kinds, that the poor boy was ready to die with fear, and begged of me not to go on shore till day.

Be that as it would, we were obliged to go on shore somewhere or other for water, for we had not a **pint**⑨ left in the boat.

人看见。我对他说："这样不行，不能这样对待主人，我们得走远一点。"他认为我这个建议并无不妥，也就同意了。他本来在船头，就扯起船帆，而我掌舵，我们一口气就把船开出将近一海里之外的水面，才把船停住，我假装要捕鱼。我把舵交给那个小孩，一步跨到那个摩尔人身边，装作要在他身后寻找什么东西的样子，我用胳膊冷不防把他拦腰一抱，一下子把他丢到了海里。

我本来可以把那个摩尔人留在身边，而把那个小孩淹死，但我信不过他。

那个孩子对我笑嘻嘻的，发誓要忠于我，随我走到天涯海角。他那种天真的神气，使我无法不相信他。

我已经被摩尔人吓破了胆，我一想到再次落入他们手中就感到非常害怕，再加上风向又顺，于是我根本不停，也不靠岸，也不下锚，就这样，我用这种方式一口气竟走了 5 天。这时风向渐渐转为南面的方向。我估计即使他们有人在后面追我，这时也要放弃了。因此，我大着胆子向岸边驶去，来到一个河口抛了描，靠了岸。

但是一到天黑，我们就听到无数野兽的可怕的咆哮声，对于这些野兽，我根本不知道是什么动物，这些声音把那个可怜的孩子吓得半死，哀求我天亮再上岸。

不管怎样，我们非得找个地方上岸，去弄点水来，因为我们的船上已经没有一点淡水了。

这次停船以后，我们一连往南走了 10 天或者

① helm /helm/ *n.* 舵，驾驶盘

② stoop /stuːp/ *v.* 弯下，弯下上身

③ toss /tɔs/ *v.* 投掷

④ venture /'ventʃə/ *v.* 冒险，*n.* 风险

⑤ anchor /'æŋkə/ *n.* 铁锚

⑥ bark /baːk/ *v.* 犬吠，叫

⑦ roar /rɔ/ *v.* 吼，咆哮

⑧ howl /haul/ *v.* 狂吠，咆哮

⑨ pint /paint/ *n.* 品脱

After this stop, we made on to the southward continually for ten or twelve days, living very sparingly on our **provisions**①, which began to abate very much, and going no oftener to the shore than we were obliged to for fresh water. My design in this was to make the river Gambia or Senegal, that is to say anywhere about the Cape de Verde, where I was in hopes to meet with some European ship; and if I did not, I knew not what course I had to take, but to seek for the islands, or **perish**② there among the negroes.

When I had pursued this resolution about ten days longer, as I have said, I began to see that the land was inhabited; and in two or three places, as we sailed by, we saw people stand upon the shore to look at us; we could also **perceive**③ they were quite black and naked.

On a sudden, the boy cried out, "Master, master, a ship with a sail!"

I jumped out of the cabin, and immediately saw, not only the ship, but that it was a Portuguese ship; and, as I thought, was bound to the coast of Guinea, for negroes. I stretched out to sea as much as I could, resolving to speak with them if possible.

As I had my patron's **ancient**④ on board, I made a **waft**⑤ of it to them, for a signal of distress, and fired a gun, both which they saw; for they told me they saw the smoke, though they did not hear the gun. Upon these signals they very kindly brought to, and lay by for me; and in about three hours time I came up with them.

It was an inexpressible joy to me, which any one will believe, that I was thus delivered, as I **esteemed**⑥ it, from such a miserable and almost hopeless condition as I was in; and I immediately offered all I had to the captain of the ship, as a return for my deliverance; but he

12天，我们吃得非常节省，因为我们的粮食日渐减少，除了不得不上岸取淡水以外，我们很少靠岸。我计划把船开到非洲海岸的冈比亚河或塞内加尔河。也就是说，我们要到佛得角一带，希望能在那里遇见一些欧洲商船。万一遇不到的话，我就不知道去哪里好了，只好去找那些岛屿，或是死在黑人堆里。

当我抱着这种决心走了大约10天时，我们就开始看到有人烟的地方了。有两三个地方，在我们经过时，我们可以看见一些人站在岸上望着我们，同时也可以看出这些人非常黑，并且周身一丝不挂。

突然之间，那个孩子叫了起来："主人，主人，一只带帆的船!"

我跳出船舱一看，立刻看出这不但是一只船，而且肯定是一艘到几内亚海岸的葡萄牙船，我想这只船一定是用来到几内亚海岸贩运黑人的。于是我拼命把船向海里开去，决定尽可能地同他们搭话。

我船上有东家的旗帜，我就把旗帜向他们摇了摇，发出求助，并且又打了一枪。这两个信号，他们都已经看到了。尽管没有听见枪声，却看见了硝烟。他们看到信号后，就停船等候我们。大约过了3个小时，我们才靠拢了他们的船。

谁都会相信，正如我自己评价它一样，我从这种困苦绝望、孤独无援的处境中得到救援，该有多么的高兴。我立刻把我所有的东西都献给了

① provision /prə'viʒən/ n. 食物，供应品

② perish /'periʃ/ v. 毁灭，死亡

③ perceive /pə'siːv/ v. 察觉，感觉

④ ancient /eiʃənt/ n. 旗子

⑤ waft /waːft/ n. 飘浮，飘荡

⑥ esteem /is'tiːm/ v. 评价，认为

generously told me he would take nothing from me, but that all I had should be delivered safe to me when I came to the Brazils. "For," says he, "I have saved your life on no other terms than I would be glad to be saved myself; and it may, one time or other, be my lot to be taken up in the same condition. Besides," said he, "when I carry you to the Brazils, so great a way from your own country, if I should take from you what you have, you will be starved there, and then I only take away that life I have given. No, no," says he: "Seignior Inglese" (Mr. Englishman), "I will carry you **thither**① in charity, and those things will help to buy your **subsistence**② there, and your passage home again."

We had a very good voyage to the Brazils, and I arrived in the Bay de Todos los Santos, or All Saints' Bay, in about twenty-two days after.

The generous treatment the captain gave me I can never enough remember.

I had not been long here before I was recommended to the house of a good honest man like himself, who had an INGENIO, as they call it—that is, a **plantation**③ and a sugar-house. I lived with him some time, and acquainted myself by that means with the manner of planting and making of sugar; and seeing how well the planters lived, and how they got rich suddenly, I resolved, if I could get a **licence**④ to settle there, I would turn planter among them, resolving in the meantime to find out some way to get my money, which I had left in London, **remitted**⑤ to me. To this purpose, getting a kind of letter of **naturalisation**⑥, I purchased as much land that was **uncured**⑦ as my money would reach, and formed a plan for my plantation and settlement; such a one as might be suitable to the **stock**⑧ which I

船主，报答他的救命之恩。但是他慷慨地对我说，他不会接受我的任何东西，等到了巴西以后，他会把我所有的一切都会完整无缺地交还我。“因为，”他说，“我救你的命，只不过是希望将来有人救我的命。说不定有一天我也会碰到同样情形哩。”除此之外，他还说：“我把你带到巴西以后，你离家乡那么远，如果我把你的东西都拿走，你一定会在那儿被饿死的。那不等于我救了你的命又要了你的命吗？”“不行，不行，英国先生，”他说，“我把你带到巴西是一种慈善行为，这些东西可以帮助你在那里生活，做你回家的盘缠。”

我们一路顺利地向巴西驶去，大约 22 天之后，我们便抵达巴西东岸的德·托德斯·劳斯·圣特斯，又叫群圣湾。

那位船长对我的好处和恩惠，真是数不胜数。

我刚到巴西不久，船长便介绍我到与他同样正直的人家里去住。这个人有一块甘蔗种植园和一座糖坊。我和他住了一段时间以后，渐渐地学会了他们种植甘蔗和制糖的方法。我见那些种植园主人的日子过得不错，发财的速度也非常之快，于是我便打定主意，只要我能获得一张居留证，我也会成为那些种植园主中的一员。同时，我还决心要想办法把我在伦敦的存款汇来。为了达到这个目的，我弄到了一张入籍的许可证，尽我所有的钱买了一块没有开垦过的土地，并且根据我将要从伦敦收到的汇款，制订了一份与这笔

① thither /ˈðiðə/ *ad.* 到那处，向那方
② subsistence /sʌbˈsistəns/ *n.* 衣食，给养
③ plantation /plænˈteiʃən/ *n.* 种植园
④ license /ˈlaisəns/ *n.* 执照，许可证
⑤ remit /riˈmit/ *v.* 汇出
⑥ naturalization /ˌnætʃərəlaiˈzeiʃən/ *n.* 归化，入籍
⑦ uncured /ʌnˈkjuəd /*a.* 未处治的
⑧ stock/stɔk/ *n.* 积蓄，储蓄

proposed to myself to receive from England.

You may suppose, that having now lived almost four years in the Brazils, and beginning to **thrive**[①] and prosper very well upon my plantation, I had not only learned the language, but had contracted acquaintance and friendship among my fellow-planters, as well as among the merchants at St. Salvador, which was our **port**[②].

In my discourses among them, I had frequently given them an account of my two voyages to the coast of Guinea: the manner of trading with the negroes there, and how easy it was to purchase upon the coast for **trifles**[③]—such as beads, toys, knives, scissors, **hatchets**[④], bits of glass, and the like—not only **gold-dust**[⑤], Guinea grains, elephants' teeth, etc., but negroes, for the service of the Brazils, in great numbers.

They listened always very attentively to my discourses on these heads, but especially to that part which related to the buying of negroes, which was a trade at that time, not only not far entered into, but, as far as it was, had been carried on by assientos, or permission of the kings of Spain and Portugal, and **engrossed**[⑥] in the public stock: so that few negroes were bought, and these excessively dear.

It happened, being in company with some merchants and planters of my acquaintance, and talking of those things very earnestly, three of them came to me next morning, and told me they had been **musing**[⑦] very much upon what I had discoursed with them of the last night, and they came to make a secret proposal to me; and, after enjoining me to secrecy, they told me that they had a mind to fit out a ship to go to Guinea; that they had all plantations as well as I, and were **straitened**[⑧] for nothing so much as servants; that as it was a trade that could not be

款子数量适合的种植和居住的计划。

你可以想像，到现在为止我已经在巴西住了差不多4年了，我的种植园事业也在蒸蒸日上、蓬勃发展。我不仅学会了当地的语言，而且在当地种植园主中间以及当地港口——圣萨尔瓦多的商人中间有了许多熟人和朋友。

在与他们聊天的时候，我经常向他们谈起我两次航行到几内亚海岸的情形，谈到怎样与那儿的黑人做生意，只要用一些小玩意，例如用一些珠子、玩具、刀具、剪子、斧子、玻璃器皿之类的东西，不但就可以换回金沙、豆蔻、象牙之类的东西，甚至可以换回在巴西大量使用的黑人，这是多么轻而易举的事情啊！

他们总是非常专心地听我讲我的这些经历，而且特别注意有关贩卖黑奴方面的知识。这种生意在那个时候还很不盛行，不过就其实际情况而言，这项贸易必须得到西班牙国王或葡萄牙国王的许可才行，并且带有垄断性质，因此黑奴进口数量也少，价钱也相当昂贵。

有一次，我非常偶然地跟几个熟识的商人和种植园主在一起，很起劲地谈论这些事情。第二天一早，他们中的3个人便来找我，告诉我说，他们非常仔细思考了一下我昨晚对他们讲述的内容，特地悄悄来向我提个建议。他们首先要求我保密，然后告诉我，他们准备弄一条船到几内亚去。他们说，他们与我的情况类似，都有自己的种植园，目前最缺乏的就是佣人。他们接着强调，他们并不想长期

① thrive /θraiv/ *v.* 兴旺，繁荣

② port /pɔːt/ *n.* 港口

③ trifle /'traifl/ *n.* 琐事，琐碎的东西

④ hatchet /'hætʃit/ *n.* 短柄小斧

⑤ gold-dust *n.*（金砂矿的）金末，金泥

⑥ engross /in'grəus/ *v.* （以垄断方式）大量收购，独占

⑦ muse /'mjuːz/ *v.* 沉思，瞑想

⑧ straitened /'streitnd/ *a.* 贫困的

carried on, because they could not publicly sell the negroes when they came home, so they desired to make but one voyage, to bring the negroes on shore privately, and divide them among their own plantations; and, in a word, the question was whether I would go their **supercargo**① in the ship, to manage the trading part upon the coast of Guinea; and they offered me that I should have my equal share of the negroes, without providing any part of the stock.

I, that was born to be my own destroyer, could no more resist the offer than I could restrain my first rambling designs when my father's good counsel was lost upon me. In a word, I told them I would go with all my heart, if they would undertake to look after my plantation in my absence, and would **dispose**② of it to such as I should direct, if I miscarried. This they all engaged to do, and entered into writings or **covenants**③ to do so.

Accordingly, the ship being fitted out, and the cargo furnished, and all things done, as by agreement, by my partners in the voyage, I went on board in an evil hour, the 1st September 1659, being the same day eight years that I went from my father and mother at Hull, in order to act the **rebel**④ to their authority, and the fool to my own interests.

The same day I went on board we set sail, standing away to the northward upon our own coast, with design to stretch over for the African coast when we came about ten or twelve degrees of northern **latitude**⑤, which, it seems, was the manner of course in those days. We had very good weather, only excessively hot.

A violent **tornado**⑥, or hurricane, took us quite out of our knowledge. It began from the south-east, came about to the north-west, and then settled in the north-east; from **whence**⑦ it blew in such a

从事这种贩卖黑奴的生意，因为回来以后不能公开出售黑奴，他们只想进行一次这样的航行，把黑奴秘密地运回来，再把他们分配到每个人的种植园中。简而言之，他们的问题就是，我愿不愿意跟他们带着大批货物乘船，到几内亚海岸去做这笔交易。他们答应我可以得到与他们一份相同数量的黑人奴隶，而且不用我掏任何钱。

我这个人生来就是自己的克星，经受不住他们这种建议的诱惑，正如当初拒绝父亲的忠告、一心一意想着要周游世界一样。总之，我告诉他们，我非常愿意去，只要他们在我离开的日子里帮我照料好我的种植园就行，并且万一在我出了事之后按照我的遗嘱来处理。这些条件，他们满口答应了，而且立了字据。

在船只准备妥当，货物筹备齐全，一切事情都与我参加航行的朋友按照合同办妥之后，我便在 1659 年 9 月 1 日那个不吉利的日子上船出海了。8 年前，我不顾一切地违背父亲和母亲的意志，愚蠢地忽视了自己的利益，从赫尔逃走，也正是这一天。

我上船的那天，我们就出海了，沿着我们自己的海岸往北航行，按照计划是横渡大洋，直达非洲海岸线。当时北纬 10 度和 12 度之间似乎是大家都要走的航线。一路上天气很好，只是太热了。

这个时候，我们忽然遇到一股强劲的飓风，真是出乎我们的意料之外，这股飓风起初来自东南方向，接着转为西北方向，最后变成东北风，

① supercargo /'sjuːpə 'kaːgəu/ *n.* 货物管理员

② dispose /dis'pəuz/ *v.* 处理，处置

③ covenant /'kʌvinənt/ *n.* 契约

④ rebel /'rebəl/ *n.* 叛徒，反叛者

⑤ latitude /'lætitjuːd/ *n.* 纬度

⑥ tornado /tɔː'neidəu/ *n.* 龙卷风

⑦ whence /(h)wens/ *ad.* 出于什么原因，从哪里

terrible manner, that for twelve days together we could do nothing but drive, and, **scudding**① away before it, let it carry us whither fate and the **fury**② of the winds directed.

In this distress, the wind still blowing very hard, one of our men early in the morning cried out, "Land!" and we had no sooner run out of the cabin to look out, in hopes of seeing whereabouts in the world we were, than the ship struck upon a **sand**③, and in a moment her motion being so stopped, the sea broke over her in such a manner that we expected we should all have perished immediately; and we were immediately driven into our close **quarters**④, to shelter us from the very **foam**⑤ and **spray**⑥ of the sea.

In this distress the mate of our vessel laid hold of the boat, and with the help of the rest of the men got her **slung**⑦ over the ship's side; and getting all into her, let go, and committed ourselves, being eleven in number, to God's mercy and the wild sea.

After we had rowed, or rather driven about a league and a half, as we **reckoned**⑧ it, a **raging**⑨ wave, mountain-like, came rolling **astern**⑩ of us, and plainly bade us expect the COUP DE GRACE. It took us with such a fury, that it overset the boat at once; and separating us as well from the boat as from one another, gave us no time to say, "O God!" for we were all swallowed up in a moment.

Nothing can describe the confusion of thought which I felt when I sank into the water; for though I swam very well, yet I could not deliver myself from the waves so as to draw breath, till that wave having driven me, or rather carried me, a vast way on towards the shore, and having spent itself, went back, and left me upon the land almost dry, but half dead with the water I took in. I had so much

来势之猛，非常可怕。就这样一连12天，我们一筹莫展，在风浪中跟着风向被卷来卷去，除了听天由命外，没有一点其他办法。

正在狂风大作的危急时刻，有一天早晨，船上有人忽然喊道："陆地！"我们刚刚跑出船舱，希望看看我们究竟到了什么地方，我们的船就搁浅在沙滩上了，再也动弹不得。滔天巨浪不断打在船身上，船就这样不停地东摇西晃，让我们感到离死亡之神并不遥远了。我们立刻躲进船舱，以此来躲避翻滚的巨浪的拍打。

在这危急万状的时刻，我们船上的大副抓住了一只小艇，在船上其他人的帮助下，我们把这只小艇拉到了大船的旁边。然后，我们11个人一齐上了小艇，把小艇解开，听凭上天和风浪去安排我们的命运吧。

与其说是我们摇着桨，不如说是被风吹着航行了一海里半的路程。忽然，排山倒海般的巨浪从我们后面赶来，显然要给我们毁灭性的打击。说时迟，那时快，我们的小艇立刻被掀了个底朝天，我们来不及喊上帝就东一个、西一个地被掀到海里，很快就被波涛吞没了。

当我沉到水里的时候，我内心的那份混乱，简直无法描绘。我虽然水性很好，但在那种惊涛骇浪中，连浮起呼吸一下都感到特别艰难。到了后来，与其说海浪把我向岸上驱赶，倒还不如说把我向岸边卷去，等它渐渐耗尽力气，退下去的时候，我被留在了半干的沙滩上，被水灌得半

① scud /skʌd/ *v.* 飞跑，刮面
② fury /'fjuəri/ *n.* 愤怒，狂暴
③ sand /sænd/ *n.* 砂，沙滩
④ quarter /'kwɔːtə/ *n.* 船（舷）的后部
⑤ foam /fəum/ *n.* 泡沫，水沫
⑥ spray /sprei/ *n.* 水沫，喷雾
⑦ sling /sliŋ/ *v.* 用吊钩钓上
⑧ reckon /'rekən/ *v.* 计算，评估
⑨ rage /reidʒ/ *v.* 发怒，震怒
⑩ astern /ə'stəːn/ *ad.* 在船尾，向船尾

presence of mind, as well as breath left, that seeing myself nearer the mainland than I expected, I got upon my feet, and endeavoured to make on towards the land as fast as I could before another wave should return and take me up again.

I was now landed and safe on shore, and began to look up and thank God that my life was saved, in a case wherein there was some minutes before **scarce**[①] any room to hope.

After I had **solaced**[②] my mind with the comfortable part of my condition, I began to look round me, to see what kind of place I was in, and what was next to be done; and I soon found my comforts abate, and that, in a word, I had a dreadful deliverance; for I was wet, had no clothes to shift me, nor anything either to eat or drink to comfort me.

All the remedy that offered to my thoughts at that time was to get up into a thick bushy tree like a **fir**[③], but **thorny**[④], which grew near me, and where I resolved to sit all night, and consider the next day what death I should die, for as yet I saw no prospect of life.

When I waked it was broad day, the weather clear, and the storm abated, so that the sea did not **rage**[⑤] and swell as before.

When I came down from my apartment in the tree, I looked about me again, and the first thing I found was the boat, which lay, as the wind and the sea had tossed her up, upon the land, about two miles on my right hand. So I came back for the present, being more **intent**[⑥] upon getting at the ship, where I hoped to find something for my present subsistence.

I pulled off my clothes—for the weather was hot to extremity—and took the water. But when I came to the ship my difficulty was still

死。幸亏此刻我的头脑还很清醒，我还有一口气，看见自己已经靠近陆地了，比预料的还要强一些，便爬起来，拼命向前跑去，免得第二个接踵而来的浪头再把我追上。

我现在已经登上了陆地，平安地上岸了，于是抬起头，感谢上天怜悯之心，因为几分钟前我还没有生还的希望。

① scarce /skεəs/ a. 缺乏的，不足的

② solace /'sɔləs/ v. 安慰，缓和

在庆幸自己不幸之中得到万幸之后，我开始环顾四周，看看自己到了什么地方，下一步该怎么办。我的情绪很快低落了下来。也就是说，我陷入了一种可怕的境地：因为我全身都被打湿了，没有衣服可换穿，同时也没有任何可以充饥止渴的东西。

这时我唯一的想法就是，爬到我附近的一颗像枞树但又有刺的枝叶茂密的大树上，在上面呆一整夜，然后第二天再考虑该怎么去死，因为我实在看不到有任何生存的希望。

③ fir /fə/ n. 枞树，枞木

④ thorny /'θɔːni/ a. 多刺的

当我醒来的时候，天已大亮了。这时天气晴朗，风暴渐渐平息了，海面上也不像先前那样波浪滔天了。

⑤ swell/swel/ v. 掀起巨浪

我从树上的栖身之处下来以后，又向四周看了看，我首先看到的第一个东西是那艘小艇，经过海上的风吹浪打之后，已被搁浅在陆地上，在我的右侧，大约有两里路。于是我暂时不打算过去，因为我现在最想到大船上去，希望能在那儿找到一些生活的必需品。

⑥ intent /in'tent/ a. 专心的，决心的

这时候，天气热极了，于是我脱了衣服，跳到水里。但是，当我游到那艘大船边的时候，我

greater to know how to get on board; for, as she lay aground, and high out of the water, there was nothing within my reach to lay hold of. I swam round her twice, and the second time I spied a small piece of rope, which I wondered I did not see at first, hung down by the fore-chains so low, as that with great difficulty I got hold of it, and by the help of that rope I got up into the **forecastle**① of the ship.

You may be sure my first work was to search, and to see what was **spoiled**② and what was free. And, first, I found that all the ship's provisions were dry and untouched by the water, and being very well disposed to eat, I went to the bread room and filled my pockets with biscuit, and ate it as I went about other things, for I had no time to lose. I also found some **rum**③ in the great cabin, of which I took a large **dram**④, and which I had, indeed, need enough of to spirit me for what was before me. Now I wanted nothing but a boat to **furnish**⑤ myself with many things which I foresaw would be very necessary to me.

It was **in vain**⑥ to sit still and wish for what was not to be had; and this extremity **roused**⑦ my application. We had several spare **yards**⑧, and two or three large **spars**⑨ of wood, and a spare **topmast**⑩ or two in the ship; I resolved to fall to work with these, and I flung as many of them overboard as I could manage for their weight, tying every one with a rope, that they might not drive away. When this was done I went down the ship's side, and pulling them to me, I tied four of them together at both ends as well as I could, in the form of a **raft**⑪, and laying two or three short pieces of **plank**⑫ upon them crossways, I found I could walk upon it very well, but that it was not able to bear any great weight, the pieces being too light. So I went to work, and with a **carpenter**'s⑬ **saw**⑭ I cut a spare topmast into three lengths, and

面临的最大困难是无法爬上去，因为船搁浅在沙滩上，离水面很高，我没有什么东西可以抓住往上爬。我绕着船游了两圈，到了第二圈时，忽然发现了一根短绳子。我暗自惊奇：为什么刚才没有发现呢？那根绳子从船头直垂下来，垂得很低，因此我很轻松地抓住了它，凭借这根绳子，我爬上了大船的前舱。

不用说，我的首要任务是看一看什么东西坏了，什么东西还没有浸水。我一眼就看到粮食都干燥无恙，并没有被水打湿。这时我感到饿了，就走进面包坊，把我的口袋都装满了饼干，一边吃着一边干着别的事，因为我必须抓紧时间才行。我还在船舱里找到了一些甘蔗酒，于是就喝了一大杯，因为在这种情况下，我非常需要喝点酒提提神。现在我什么也不想要，只想能有一只小艇，把我预见到将来所需要的东西运到岸上去。

一个人呆坐着空想是徒劳无益的。这个绝对的真理，让我重新振作了起来。船上有几根多余的帆杠，还有两三块木板，另外还有一两根多余的第二接桅。我决定先从这些东西着手，只要能搬得动的，能搬动多少，就搬多少，都把它们从船上扔了下来，每根上面都绑上绳子，以免被水冲走。这些做好以后，我把它们拉到我跟前来，把 4 块木头绑在一起，两边尽可能绑紧，扎成一只木排的样子，又把两三块短木板搁在上面。我试着在上面走了走，还可以，不过木板太轻，难以承受太重的东西。于是我又开始工作，用木匠

① forecastle /ˈfəuksl/ *n.* 前甲板下面的水手舱，船头的船楼
② spoil /spɔil/ *v.* 破坏，腐坏
③ rum /rʌm/ *n.* 甜酒
④ dram /dræm/ *n.* 一口
⑤ furnish /ˈfəːniʃ/ *v.* 供给，装设
⑥ in vain 徒然，白费
⑦ rouse /rauz/ *v.* 唤醒，鼓舞
⑧ yard /jaːd/ *n.* 帆杠
⑨ spar /spa/ *n.* 帆桅，樯
⑩ topmast /ˈtɔpmaːst/ *n.* 中桅
⑪ raft /raːft/ *n.* 筏
⑫ plank /plæŋk/ *n.* 厚木板
⑬ carpenter /ˈkaːpintə/ *n.* 木匠
⑭ saw /sɔ/ *n.* 锯子

added them to my raft, with a great deal of labour and pains. But the hope of furnishing myself with necessaries encouraged me to go beyond what I should have been able to have done upon another occasion.

My raft was now strong enough to bear any reasonable weight. My next care was what to load it with, and how to preserve what I laid upon it from the **surf**① of the sea; but I was not long considering this. I first laid all the planks or boards upon it that I could get, and having considered well what I most wanted, I got three of the seamen's **chests**②, which I had broken open, and emptied, and lowered them down upon my raft; the first of these I filled with provisions—viz. bread, rice, three Dutch cheeses, five pieces of dried goat's flesh, which we lived much upon, and a little remainder of European corn, which had been laid by for some **fowls**③ which we brought to sea with us, but the fowls were killed.

I found enough clothes, but took no more than I wanted for present use, for I had others things which my eye was more upon—as, first, tools to work with on shore. And it was after long searching that I found out the carpenter's chest, which was, indeed, a very useful prize to me, and much more valuable than a shipload of gold would have been at that time.

My next care was for some **ammunition**④ and arms. There were two very good **fowling-pieces**⑤ in the great cabin, and two pistols. These I secured first, with some powder-horns and a small bag of shot, and two old rusty swords.

I had three encouragements—1st, a smooth, calm sea; 2ndly, the tide rising, and setting in to the shore; 3rdly, what little wind there was blew me towards the land. And thus, having found two or three broken

的锯子把一根第二接桅锯成3段，把它们加在木排上。这项工作非常辛苦，但由于我非常迫切想把有用的东西运到岸上去，这就鼓舞着我做出了平常所做不出的事情。

我的木排此时已相当牢固，能够承受住有分量的东西。我的下一步就是考虑把什么东西装上去，并且如何防止这些东西被海水打湿。我很快就有了办法。我首先把船上所能找到的木板都铺了上去，然后考虑了一下我最需要什么。我把3只船员用的箱子打开，把里面的东西倒了出来，把它们吊在我的木排上。在第一只箱子里，我装了许多粮食，诸如面包、米、3块荷兰奶酪，5块羊肉干这些以前我赖以为生的东西，以及原来喂养船上一些家禽而剩下的一些欧洲麦子（这些家禽都已经死了）。

我在船上找到了许多衣服，但我只取了几件目前要用的，因为我还有一些最重要的东西要找，尤其是岸上干活要用的工具。我找了好半天，才终于找到了木匠的箱子。这些东西对我来说实在是非常有用，就算此时此刻有满满一船金子，其价值都远远比不上这些东西。

我随后想找到的是弹药和枪械。我首先从船舱里找到了两枝很好的鸟枪和两把信号枪，又拿了几只装火药的角筒、一小包子弹和两把生了锈的刀剑。

我有3点有利因素：第一，海面平静；第二，潮水正在上涨，正在向岸上冲去；第三，虽然有

① surf /səːf/ *n.* 海浪

② chest /tʃest/ *n.* 衣柜

③ fowl /faul/ *n.* 家禽

④ ammunition /ˌæmju'niʃən/ *n.* 军火，弹药

⑤ fowling-pieces *n.* 猎枪；鸟枪

oars[1] belonging to the boat—and, besides the tools which were in the chest, I found two saws, an axe, and a hammer.

My next work was to view the country, and seek a proper place for my habitation, and where to **stow**[2] my goods to secure them from whatever might happen.

There was a hill not above a mile from me, which rose up very **steep**[3] and high, and which seemed to overtop some other hills, which lay as in a **ridge**[4] from it northward. I took out one of the fowling-pieces, and one of the pistols, and a horn of powder; and thus armed, I travelled for discovery up to the top of that hill, where, after I had with great labour and difficulty got to the top, I saw any fate, to my great **affliction**[5]—viz. that I was in an island **environed**[6] every way with the sea: no land to be seen except some rocks, which lay a great way off; and two small islands, less than this, which lay about three leagues to the west.

I found also that the island I was in was **barren**[7], and, as I saw good reason to believe, uninhabited except by wild beasts, of whom, however, I saw none. Yet I saw **abundance**[8] of fowls, but knew not their kinds; neither when I killed them could I tell what was fit for food, and what not.

Contented with this discovery, I came back to my raft, and fell to work to bring my cargo on shore.

I **barricaded**[9] myself round with the chest and boards that I had brought on shore, and made a kind of **hut**[10] for that night's lodging.

I now began to consider that I might yet get a great many things out of the ship which would be useful to me, and particularly some of the **rigging**[11] and sails, and such other things as might come to land;

点微风，却是往岸上吹的。同时，我又在船上找到了两三只断桨，并除了箱子里的工具之外，又找到了两把锯，一把斧子，一把锤子。

我的下一步工作就是查看地形，找一个合适的地方来安置自己的住所，来贮藏自己的东西，预防意外的事情发生。

在距我不到一英里的地方，有一座又高又陡的小山，在它北边还有一连串的小山，好像一道山脉，但都没有它高。我在身上带了一枝鸟枪，一把手枪和一角筒火药，武装完毕之后，朝这个山顶进发。当我历尽艰辛才爬上山顶以后，我不禁开始发愁了。我发现命运对来说真是太过刻薄了。原来我到了一个海岛上，四周大海环绕，看不见一点陆地，只有很远的地方有几块礁岩，此外就是在 3 海里之外的西边，有两个比这个岛还小的岛屿。

我还发现我所在的这座海岛非常荒凉，论理来讲，这里没有人烟，大概只有野兽。我虽然没有看到野兽，却看见许多飞鸟，可是不知道它们是些什么飞禽，也不知道打死之后能不能吃。

我对于自己这次巡视颇为满意，于是回到木排旁边，动手把我的东西搬上了岸。

我把运到岸上来的那些箱子、板子，在周围堆成了一个防御工事，堆成一个类似木头房子的东西，作为夜间歇宿之用。

这时我又开始想到，我还可以从船上找出许多对我也许有用的东西，特别是那些绳索、帆布

① oar /ɔː/ *n.* 桨，橹

② stow /stəu/ *v.* 收藏起来

③ steep /stiːp/ *a.* 险峻的，陡峭的

④ ridge /ridʒ/ *n.* 脊，山脊

⑤ affliction /ə'flikʃən/ *n.* 痛苦，苦难

⑥ environ /in'vaiərən/ *v.* 包围，环绕

⑦ barren /'bærən/ *a.* 不育的，贫瘠的

⑧ abundance /ə'bʌndəns/ *n.* 丰富，充裕

⑨ barricade /ˌbæri'keid/ *v.* 防卫工事，障碍

⑩ hut /hʌt/ *n.* 小屋，棚屋

⑪ rigging /'rigiŋ/ *n.* 索具，绳索

and I resolved to make another voyage on board the vessel, if possible. And as I knew that the first storm that blew must necessarily break her all in pieces, I resolved to set all other things apart till I had got everything out of the ship that I could get.

I got on board the ship as before, and prepared a second raft; and, having had experience of the first, I neither made this so **unwieldy**①, nor loaded it so hard, but yet I brought away several things very useful to me.

But that which comforted me more still, was, that last of all, after I had made five or six such voyages as these, and thought I had nothing more to expect from the ship that was worth my **meddling with**②—I say, after all this, I found a great **hogshead**③ of bread, three large **runlets**④ of rum, or spirits, a box of sugar, and a **barrel**⑤ of fine flour.

I had been now thirteen days on shore, and had been eleven times on board the ship, in which time I had brought away all that one pair of hands could well be supposed capable to bring; though I believe **verily**⑥, had the calm weather held, I should have brought away the whole ship, piece by piece. But preparing the twelfth time to go on board, I found the wind began to rise; however, at low water I went on board, and though I thought I had **rummaged**⑦ the cabin so effectually that nothing more could be found, yet I discovered a locker with drawers in it, in one of which I found two or three razors, and one pair of large scissors, with some ten or a dozen of good knives and forks; in another I found about thirty-six pounds value in money—some European coin, some Brazil, some pieces of eight, some gold, and some silver.

I smiled to myself at the sight of this money: "O drug! " said I,

以及像这样的其他东西，它们在陆上可能用得着。因此，我决定，如果可能的话，我再到船上去一次。我知道，如果再来一次大风，一定会把船打得粉身碎骨。所以，我想先把别的事搁在一边，等我把船上能搬的东西都搬下来再说。

我像上回一样上了船，又制作了一只木排。因为有了第一次的经验，我没有再把木排做得那样笨重，也没有堆放太多的东西，但还是从船上搬了不少有用的东西下来。

① unwieldy /ʌn'wiːldi/ a. 笨重的，笨拙的

然而最使我感到欣慰的是，最终我这样来来回回跑了五六趟之后，我以为船上已经没有什么东西值得我劳神费力的时候，我是说，在所有这些努力之后，我又找到了一大桶面包，3 大桶甜酒或烈性酒、一箱糖和一桶上等的面粉。

② meddle with 乱动（他人之物）
③ hogshead /'hɔgzhed/ n. 大桶
④ runlet /'rʌnlit/ n. 桶
⑤ barrel /'bærəl/ n. 桶

我现在已经上岸 13 天，先后到船上去过 11 次。在此期间，我已经把我用我的双手所能够搬动的东西统统搬了下来。我相信，如果天气不错的话，我一定可以把整条船一块一块地搬到岸上来。但是，当我准备第 12 次上船时，就开始刮起了风。尽管如此，我还是在退潮的时候上了船。虽然我以为自己搜遍了整个船，什么也不会找到了，可是最终我又发现了一个带抽屉的柜子。在一个抽屉里，我找到了两三把剃刀、一把大剪刀、十几把刀子和叉子。而在另外一个抽屉里，我找到了许多钱币，有欧洲的、巴西的、西班牙的，有金币还有银币，大约总共值 36 英镑。

⑥ verily /'verili/ ad. 肯定地，真实的

⑦ rummage /'rʌmidʒ/ v. 到处翻寻，搜出

看见这些钱，我忍不住笑了，大声喊道：

aloud, "what art thou good for? Thou art not worth to me-no, not the taking off the ground; one of those knives is worth all this **heap**①; I have no manner of use for thee—e'en remain where thou art, and go to the bottom as a creature whose life is not worth saving." However, upon second thoughts I took it away.

I soon found the place I was in was not fit for my settlement, because it was upon a low, **moorish**② ground, near the sea, and I believed it would not be **wholesome**③, and more particularly because there was no fresh water near it; so I resolved to find a more healthy and more convenient spot of ground.

I consulted several things in my situation, which I found would be proper for me: 1st, health and fresh water, I just now mentioned; 2ndly, shelter from the heat of the sun; 3rdly, security from **ravenous**④ creatures, whether man or beast; 4thly, a view to the sea, that if God sent any ship in sight, I might not lose any advantage for my deliverance, of which I was not willing to **banish**⑤ all my expectation yet.

In search of a place proper for this, I found a little plain on the side of a rising hill, whose front towards this little plain was steep as a house-side, so that nothing could come down upon me from the top. On the one side of the rock there was a **hollow**⑥ place, worn a little way in, like the entrance or door of a cave, but there was not really any cave or way into the rock at all. On the flat of the green, just before this hollow place, I resolved to **pitch**⑦ my tent.

Before I set up my tent I drew a half-circle before the hollow place.

In this half-circle I pitched two rows of strong **stakes**⑧, driving them into the ground till they stood very firm like piles, the biggest end being

“废物！你现在还有什么用处呢？对我而言，你什么都不是，连粪土都不如。那把刀子就比你值钱。我现在用不着你，你就留在老地方，永远沉到海底去吧。我可不想拯救你。”但是，我沉思了片刻，还是把它们拿走了。

我很快就发现，我所待的地方根本不适合我居住，由于靠近大海，地势低而潮湿，我也相信这并不是很卫生，特别是附近没有淡水。因此，我决定找一个比较卫生、比较方便的地方。

根据自己的情况，我决定自己要选择的地点必须符合以下几个条件：第一，要卫生，要有我刚才提到的淡水；第二，要能在阳光遮阴；第三，要能躲避凶猛的动物，无论是野人还是野兽；第四，要能看见大海，万一有什么船只经过时，我不至于丧失脱险的机会，因为我始终不愿意放弃这个念头。

在寻找这样一个地点的时候，我找到了一个靠近小山坡的平地。那座小山前壁几乎像一堵墙一样陡峭，任何动物都无法从山顶上下来袭击我；在这座小山的前面，有一块平坦的草地，就像一个洞穴入口或者是门，但是，事实上，并没有任何洞穴，也没有通往小山的路径。我决定在这里支起我的帐篷。

在我支起帐篷之前，我在那块空地的前面划了一个半圆形。

沿着这个半圆轨迹，我插进了两排很结实的木头，把它们牢牢地钉在地里，就像木桩一样，这些

① heap /hiːp/ *n.* 堆

② moorish /ˈmuəriʃ/ *a.* 沼地的

③ wholesome /ˈhəulsəm/ *a.* 有益健康的，合乎卫生的

④ ravenous /ˈrævinəs/ *a.* 贪婪的，渴望的

⑤ banish /ˈbæniʃ/ *v.* 驱逐

⑥ hollow /ˈhɔləu/ *a.* 空的，凹的

⑦ pitch /pitʃ/ *v.* 扎牢

⑧ stake /steik/ *n.* 木柱

out of the ground above five feet and a half, and sharpened on the top. The two rows did not stand above six inches from one another.

Then I took the pieces of **cable**[①] which I had cut in the ship, and laid them in rows, one upon another, within the circle, between these two rows of stakes, up to the top, placing other stakes in the inside, leaning against them, about two feet and a half high, like a **spur**[②] to a post; and this fence was so strong, that neither man nor beast could get into it or over it.

The entrance into this place I made to be, not by a door, but by a short ladder to go over the top; which ladder, when I was in, I lifted over after me; and so I was completely fenced in and **fortified**[③], as I thought, from all the world, and consequently slept secure in the night.

Into this fence or fortress, with infinite labour, I carried all my riches, all my provisions, ammunition, and stores, of which you have the account above; and I made a large tent, which to preserve me from the rains.

When I had done this, I began to work my way into the rock, and bringing all the earth and stones that I dug down out through my tent, I laid them up within my fence, in the nature of a **terrace**[④], so that it raised the ground within about a foot and a half; and thus I made me a cave, just behind my tent, which served me like a **cellar**[⑤] to my house.

It cost me much labour and many days before all these things were brought to perfection.

In the **interval**[⑥] of time while this was doing, I went out once at least every day with my gun, as well to **divert**[⑦] myself as to see if I could kill anything fit for food; and, as near as I could, to acquaint myself with what the island produced.

木头全部是大头朝下，高出地面约5英尺半，顶上削得特别尖。两排之间的距离，不过6英寸。

然后，我又拿出我从船上割下来的缆绳，我把它们一个一个地按排放好，沿着半圆形，把两排木桩一圈一圈缠绕起来，一直到顶上，又把一些木桩放在两排木桩中间，互相支撑着，大概有2英尺半高，就像马刺一样，这样的篱笆，异常牢固，不管是人还是兽，都无法跨过或爬进来。

至于进出口，我没有做门，只用一架短梯子从顶上翻进来，进来之后，就把梯子提上来收起。这样，我被完全地围起来，正如我想的，我四面都有了保护，完全与外界隔离开来，因而晚上可以高枕无忧了。

我费了很大的力气，把以上我所讲到的全部财产——所有的粮食、军火以及贮藏品，都搬到这个篱笆或堡垒里面来。我还搭了一个大帐篷用来防雨。

完成这些工作以后，我就开始开凿那座岩壁，我把挖出来的石块和泥土从我的帐篷中运了出来，沿着篱笆后面堆起来，堆成一个围墙的样子，离地面大约有1英尺半高。这样，我就在我的背后挖了一个山洞，它可以用作我的地窖。

这些事情，我费了很大的劲，花了许多时间才完善成功。

在做这些事情的间歇，我带着枪每天至少要出去一次，一则是为了出去散散心，二则是想看看能不能打点什么可以吃的东西，同时也要了解一下岛上有什么出产。

① cable /ˈkeibl/ *n.* 麻绳

② spur /spə/ *n.* 马刺，树根

③ fortify /ˈfɔːtifai/ *v.* 设要塞，加强

④ terrace /ˈterəs/ *n.* 台地，梯田

⑤ cellar /ˈselə/ *n.* 地窖，地下室

⑥ interval /ˈintəvəl/ *n.* 间隔

⑦ divert /diˈvəːt/ *v.* 转移

The first time I went out, I presently discovered that there were goats in the island, which was a great satisfaction to me; but then it was attended with this misfortune to me—viz. that they were so shy, so subtle, and so **swift**① of foot, that it was the most difficult thing in the world to come at them; but I was not discouraged at this, not doubting but I might now and then shoot one, as it soon happened.

Having now fixed my habitation, I found it absolutely necessary to provide a place to make a fire in, and **fuel**② to burn.

And now being about to enter into a melancholy relation of a scene of silent life, such, perhaps, as was never heard of in the world before, I shall take it from its beginning, and continue it in its order.

After I had been there about ten or twelve days, it came into my thoughts that I should lose my reckoning of time for want of books and pen and ink, and should even forget the Sabbath days from the working days; but to prevent this, I cut with my knife upon a large post, in capital letters—and making it into a great cross, I set it up on the shore where I first landed—"I came on shore here on the 30th September 1659." Upon the sides of this square post I cut every day a **notch**③ with my knife, and every seventh notch was as long again as the rest, and every first day of the month as long again as that long one; and thus I kept my **calendar**④, or weekly, monthly, and yearly reckoning of time.

In the next place, we are to observe that among the many things which I brought out of the ship, in the several voyages which, as above mentioned, I made to it, I got several things of less value, but not at all less useful to me, which I **omitted**⑤ setting down before; as, in particular, pens, ink, and paper, several parcels in the captain's,

我第一次出去的时候就发现岛上有许多山羊，这使我心里非常满意。但令我感到沮丧的是，那些山羊非常胆小，非常狡猾，而且跑得非常快，想要接近它们，实在是一件非常困难的事。然而，我并没因此就产生灰心丧气的情绪，我相信迟早会捕到一只。这件事不久就应验了。

现在把住处安置好之后，我觉得非常有必要找一个生火的地方，并且要弄些柴来烧。

现在我要过一种孤独郁闷的生活了，这也许是人们以前从来没有听到过的事，因此，我要把这种经历要从头到尾、按着次序记录下来。

在我上岸大约十一二天之后，一个想法忽然闪现在我的脑子里，既然我缺少书、笔和墨水，我一定会忘记日期，甚至连安息日和工作日都会忘记。为了避免发生这种事，我便用刀子在一根大柱子上刻上了这样几个大字："我于1659年9月30日在此上岸，"并且把柱子做成了一个大十字架，立在我首次登岸的地方。在这个方柱的两边，我每天都用刀子刻一个V形凹痕，每7天刻一个大一倍的V形凹痕，每个月再刻一个更大一倍的V形凹痕。这样，我就有了一个日历，可以记住年月日了。

紧接着应该提到的是，正如我在前面所提到的，我来来回回好几次从船上搬下来许多东西，在那堆东西里面，我找到了一些价值不大而用处却不小的东西，这些都是以前在迁新居时仍掉的地图，特别是那些笔、墨水、纸及船主和大副的

① swift /swift/ *a.* 快的，迅速的

② fuel /fjuəl/ *n.* 燃料，木炭

③ notch /nɔtʃ/ *n.* 刻痕

④ calendar /'kæləndə/ *n.* 日历

⑤ omit /əu'mit/ *v.* 省略，疏忽

mate's, gunner's and carpenter's keeping; three or four **compasses**①, some mathematical instruments, dials, perspectives, charts, and books of navigation, all which I **huddled**② together, whether I might want them or no.

And I must not forget that we had in the ship a dog and two cats, of whose **eminent**③ history I may have occasion to say something in its place; for I carried both the cats with me; and as for the dog, he jumped out of the ship of himself, and swam on shore to me the day after I went on shore with my first cargo, and was a trusty servant to me many years.

As I observed before, I found pens, ink, and paper, and I **husbanded**④ them to the utmost; and I shall show that while my ink lasted, I kept things very exact, but after that was gone I could not, for I could not make any ink by any means that I could devise.

I now began to consider seriously my condition, and the circumstances I was reduced to; and I drew up the state of my affairs in writing, not so much to leave them to any that were to come after me—for I was likely to have but few **heirs**⑤—as to deliver my thoughts from daily **poring**⑥ over them, and afflicting my mind; and as my reason began now to master my **despondency**⑦, I began to comfort myself as well as I could, and to set the good against the evil, that I might have something to **distinguish**⑧ my case from worse; and I stated very **impartially**⑨, like debtor and creditor, the comforts I enjoyed against the miseries I suffered.

Having now brought my mind a little to **relish**⑩ my condition, and **given over**⑪ looking out to sea, to see if I could spy a ship—I say,

几包东西，像3、4个罗盘，一些数学仪器、日规，望远镜、地图、航海书籍等等。我当时把这些东西都收在了一起，不管是有用还是无用。

有一件不应该忘记的事情就是，我们船上还有一条狗和两只猫，我以后还会偶尔讲到它们从前的充满敌意的故事。我把那两只猫带到了岸上，那条狗是在我第一次搬东西上岸后，自动跳下船游到岸上的，后来成了我多年忠实的随从。

自从我找到笔、墨水、纸以后，我极尽节省之能。事实证明，如果我有墨水，就可以把事情记得非常清楚，如果墨水用完了，我就难以为继了，因为用我发明的任何方法都造不出墨水来。

我现在开始很认真地考虑我目前的处境，把自己的经历一一记录下来。我这样做，并非留给后来人看，因为我不相信以后还会有人来到这个荒岛上，只不过把我的思想表达出来，写出来自己看看，减轻一点心中的苦闷罢了。我的理智现在已经开始战胜了我的沮丧，开始尽量安慰自己，把当前的好处与坏处加以比较，这能够使我目前的状况不至于变得更糟，使自己能够知足安乐。于是，我仿照借方与贷方的格式以非常公正地方式表达出来，把我的不幸与幸运列出来。

我现在对自己的处境多少有了些好感，不再整天盯着海面，等待有什么船只经过。我是说，我已经把这些事情丢在了一边，开始一心一意过日子，

① compass /'kʌmpəs/ *n.* 指南针

② huddle /'hʌdl/ *v.* 推挤，乱堆

③ eminent /'eminənt/ *a.* 著名的，卓越的

④ husband /'hʌzbənd/ *v.* 节俭地使用

⑤ heir /ɛə/ *n.* 继承人

⑥ pore /pɔ/ *v.* 熟视，细想

⑦ despondency /di'spɔndənsi/ *n.* 失去勇气，失望

⑧ distinguish /dis'tiŋgwiʃ/ *v.* 区别

⑨ impartially /im'pa:ʃəli/ *ad.* 公平地，无私地

⑩ relish /'reliʃ/ *v.* 品味，喜欢

⑪ give over 不再，停止

giving over these things, I begun to apply myself to arrange my way of living, and to make things as easy to me as I could.

I have already described my habitation, which was a tent under the side of a rock, surrounded with a strong pale of posts and cables, but I might now rather call it a wall, for I raised a kind of wall up against it of **turfs**[①], about two feet thick on the outside; and after some time, I think it was a year and a half, I raised rafters from it, leaning to the rock, and **thatched**[②] or covered it with **boughs**[③] of trees, and such things as I could get, to keep out the rain, which I found at some times of the year very violent.

And now I began to apply myself to make such necessary things as I found I most wanted, particularly a chair and a table; for without these I was not able to enjoy the few comforts I had in the world; I could not write or eat, or do several things, with so much pleasure without a table.

Some days after this, and after I had been on board the ship, and got all that I could out of her, yet I could not forbear getting up to the top of a little mountain and looking out to sea, in hopes of seeing a ship; then **fancy**[④] at a vast distance I spied a sail, please myself with the hopes of it, and then after looking steadily, till I was almost blind, lose it quite, and sit down and **weep**[⑤] like a child, and thus increase my misery by my folly.

But having gotten over these things in some measure, and having settled my household staff and habitation, made me a table and a chair, and all as handsome about me as I could, I began to keep my journal; for having no more ink, I was forced to leave it off.

During this time I made my rounds in the woods for **game**[⑥] every

尽量改善自己的生活，尽我所能而随遇而安。

我已经描述过我的住所。这是一个搭在岩石一侧下面、四周被用木桩和缆绳做成的坚固的木栅所环绕的帐篷。我现在可以称这个木栅为墙了，因为我已用草皮在外面堆成了一道2尺来厚的墙，过了一些时日，我想大约是一年半以后，在它与岩壁间搭了一些屋椽，上面盖了些树皮和一些别的可以弄得到的东西，来挡住雨水，因为每年总有一段时间雨水很大。

① turf /təːf/ *n.* 草地
② thatch /θætʃ/ *v.* 用草铺盖屋顶
③ bough /bau/ *n.* 大树枝

我现在着手制作一些我所发现的最紧迫需要的，而且是生活中必不可少的东西，特别是桌子、椅子；因为假使没有这些东西，我就不能如此快乐地写字、吃饭或做其他事情，也就无法享受世上的乐趣。

几天之后，我把船上所有能够搬动的东西都搬走以后，还是不由自主地整天爬到那小山的顶上，呆呆地望着海面，企盼能看到一只船。有时我幻觉出远处出现了一片帆影，我非常高兴，以为有救了，于是望了又望，把眼都看花了，却没有。于是，我坐在地上，像孩子似的大哭。我的愚蠢增加了我的痛苦。

④ fancy /ˈfænsi/ *v.* 想像，幻想
⑤ weep /wiːp/ *v.* 哭泣，流泪

但是，这个阶段过去之后，在我把自己的住所及物品安排妥当，为自己制作了一张桌子、一把椅子，并把一切整理完毕之后，我就开始记起日记来。因为后来墨水没有了，我不得不终止。

在这些日子里，只要不下雨，我总是要到小树林去走走转转，在这种散步中，我经常会有所

⑥ game /geim/ *n.* 猎物

day when the rain permitted me, and made frequent discoveries in these walks of something or other to my advantage.

In the middle of all my labours it happened that, rummaging my things, I found a little bag which, as I hinted before, had been filled with corn for the feeding of **poultry**①—not for this voyage, but before, as I suppose, when the ship came from Lisbon. The little remainder of corn that had been in the bag was all **devoured**② by the rats, and I saw nothing in the bag but **husks**③ and dust; and being willing to have the bag for some other use, I think it was to put powder in, when I divided it for fear of the lightning, or some such use, I shook the husks of corn out of it on one side of my fortification, under the rock.

I threw this stuff away, taking no notice, and not so much as remembering that I had thrown anything there, when, about a month after, or **thereabouts**④, I saw some few stalks of something green shooting out of the ground, which I fancied might be some plant I had not seen; but I was surprised, and perfectly astonished, when, after a little longer time, I saw about ten or twelve **ears**⑤ come out, which were perfect green **barley**⑥, of the same kind as our European—nay, as our English barley.

This touched my heart a little, and brought tears out of my eyes, and I began to bless myself that such a **prodigy**⑦ of nature should happen upon my account; and this was the more strange to me, because I saw near it still, all along by the side of the rock, some other **straggling**⑧ stalks, which proved to be stalks of rice, and which I knew, because I had seen it grow in Africa when I was ashore there.

At last it occurred to my thoughts that I shook a bag of chickens' meat out in that place; and then the wonder began to **cease**⑨.

发现，或者找到一些对我有用的东西。

在我工作过程中，我偶然翻寻我的东西，找到了一个小布袋。我曾提到，这个布袋原来装的是喂养家禽的谷物，并且不是为此次旅行所准备的，我猜想可能是上次从里斯本出发时带来的。袋子里的一点谷物早已被老鼠打了牙祭了，我在袋子中只找到了一点尘土与谷皮。我记得，当我害怕雷电而把火药分开的时候，曾用它装过火药或诸如此类的用处。现在我想把布袋派别的用场，于是就把那点谷皮抖在岩石下面的围墙里面。

当我把这些东西倒掉的时候，当时一点也没有在意，甚至连扔东西这件事都忘记了。不料过了一个多月，我忽然看见地上抽出了几根绿色植物的茎叶。我刚开始还以为是自己过去没有注意的什么草类，不料过了不太长的时间以后，我却大为惊讶，因为我看见那些茎子上又长出十几颗穗子，这的确是大麦穗子，与欧洲的大麦完全属于同一个品种，甚至和我们英国的品种都一样。

这使我不由得落下泪来，心里颇为感动。我开始暗自庆幸，庆幸天地间还有这种怪事出现在我的身边。对我来说更怪的是，在离那块岩石一侧不远的地方，我又看到几根稀疏的绿茎，显然是稻茎，这是我所知道的，因为我在非洲岸上曾看到过这种稻子。

最后，我终于想起来了，我曾经把一袋鸡食饲料倒在那里，想到这个，我这才不再惊讶了。

不用多说，6月底左右就是收获的季节，我

① poultry /ˈpəultri/ *n.* 家禽

② devour /diˈvauə/ *v.* 吞食

③ husk /hʌsk/ *n.* 外壳，皮

④ thereabouts /ˈðεərəbauts/ *ad.* 在那附近，大约

⑤ ear /iə/ *n.* 穗

⑥ barley /ˈbaːli/ *n.* 大麦

⑦ prodigy /ˈprɔdidʒi/ *n.* 惊人的事物

⑧ straggle /ˈstrægl/ *v.* 分散，零零落落

⑨ cease /siːs/ *v.* 停止，终了

I carefully saved the ears of this corn, you may be sure, in their season, which was about the end of June; and, laying up every corn, I resolved to sow them all again, hoping in time to have some quantity **sufficient**[①] to supply me with bread. But it was not till the fourth year that I could allow myself the least grain of this corn to eat, and even then but sparingly.

I had now been in this unhappy island above ten months. All possibility of deliverance from this condition seemed to be entirely taken from me; and I firmly believe that no human shape had ever set foot upon that place. Having now secured my habitation, as I thought, fully to my mind, I had a great desire to make a more perfect discovery of the island, and to see what other productions I might find, which I yet knew nothing of.

I found different fruits, and particularly I found **melons**[②] upon the ground, in great abundance, and grapes upon the trees. The vines had spread, indeed, over the trees, and the **clusters**[③] of grapes were just now in their prime, very ripe and rich. This was a surprising discovery, and I was exceeding glad of them.

I found an excellent use for these grapes; and that was, to cure or dry them in the sun, and keep them as dried grapes or raisins are kept, which I thought would be, as indeed they were, wholesome and agreeable to eat when no grapes could be had.

I saw here abundance of cocoa trees, orange, and lemon, and **citron**[④] trees; but all wild, and very few bearing any fruit, at least not then.

I found now I had business enough to gather and carry home; and I resolved to lay up a store as well of grapes as limes and lemons, to

小心翼翼地把这些谷物穗子保存了起来。我把每粒种子都放好，准备把它们再种一下，希望将来收获多了，可以用来制作面包。不过一直到第四年头上，我才吃到一点谷物，并且依旧吃得很节省。

① sufficient /sə'fiʃənt/ *a.* 足够的，充分的

我来到这个不幸的岛屿上已经10个多月了。对我而言，所有摆脱目前这种困境的可能性似乎不复存在了，而且我坚信，人类的足迹从来没有踏上过这块土地。我想我现在的住处完全遂我心愿。我非常想要做的事，就是对这个岛屿做一次更全面的了解，看看还有什么我所不知道的其他出产。

我发现岛上有许多不同的水果，特别是地上长着各种各样的瓜类，数量非常丰富，树上布满了葡萄藤，挂满了一串又一串的葡萄，这时正是葡萄长得最好的时候，又熟又大。这真是一个意外的发现，我感到非常高兴。

② melon /'melən/ *n.* 甜瓜

③ cluster /'klʌstə/ *n.* 串，丛

对于这些葡萄，我想出了一个极好的法子，那就是把它们放在太阳下面晒干，做成葡萄干来贮藏。我相信等到没有葡萄的时候来吃，这些东西就像我以前吃的那样，一定又滋养又可口。

我又看到许多椰子树、桔子树、柠檬树和橙子树，不过都是野生的，很少结果子，至少那时是如此。

④ citron /'sitrən/ *n.* 香木缘

我发现现在有许多事要做，要把这些东西收起来搬回家。我决定把诸如葡萄、白柠檬和柠檬这些果子贮藏起来，作为我雨季的食物。我知道

furnish myself for the wet season, which I knew was approaching.

I saw abundance of parrots, and **fain**① I would have caught one, if possible, to have kept it to be tame, and taught it to speak to me. I did, after some **painstaking**②, catch a young parrot, for I knocked it down with a stick, and having recovered it, I brought it home; but it was some years before I could make him speak; however, at last I taught him to call me by name very familiarly.

I found in the low grounds **hares**③, as I thought them to be, and foxes; but they differed greatly from all the other kinds I had met with, nor could I satisfy myself to eat them, though I killed several. But I had no need to be **venturous**④, for I had no want of food, and of that which was very good too, especially these three sorts, viz. goats, pigeons, and turtle, or **tortoise**⑤, which added to my grapes, Leadenhall market could not have furnished a table better than I, **in proportion to**⑥ the company.

My dog surprised a young kid, and seized upon it; and I, running in to take hold of it, caught it, and saved it alive from the dog. I had a great mind to bring it home if I could, for I had often been musing whether it might not be possible to get a kid or two, and so raise a breed of tame goats, which might supply me when my powder and shot should be all spent.

As I continually fed it, the creature became so loving, so gentle, and so fond, that it became from that time one of my **domestics**⑦ also, and would never leave me afterwards.

I was now, in the months of November and December, expecting my crop of barley and rice.

I was sadly put to it for a **scythe**⑧ or **sickle**⑨ to cut it down, and all

雨季很快就要来了。

我又看见许多鹦鹉，很想捉一只，如果有可能的话，把它驯养起来，教它和我说话。我费了不少周折，才用棍子打下一只小鹦鹉，等它苏醒以后，把它带回了家。教会这只小鹦鹉说话，是几年以后的事情，可是，我终于教会了它如何很亲热地叫我的名字。

我在低地里看见了许多像野兔一样的东西，还有许多狐狸，但它们与我所见过的其他种类的狐狸大不相同。尽管我打死了几只，却不想吃它们的肉，我无须冒险，因为我并不缺少食物，而且我的食物很好，尤其是山羊、鸽子和鳖这 3 种食物。再加上我的葡萄干，恐怕就是伦敦利登厅这样物品丰足的市场也配不出一桌比我目前餐桌上更为丰盛的筵席，当然这仅就吃饭人数而言。

我的狗袭击了一只小山羊，咬住了小羊。我急忙跑过去把它从狗嘴里抢救下来。我想，如果可能的话，就把它带回去，因为我经常考虑能不能弄到一两只小羊，用来繁殖出一群驯养的羊，这样一旦我的弹药用完时可供我享用。

后来，由于我不断地喂它，这只小山羊变得又可爱又温和，它成了我的家畜中的一员，再也离不开我了。

现正处于 11 月和 12 月之间，我正盼望着收获我的大麦和稻米。

这时我最感不便的是缺少一把割庄稼的镰刀，

① fain /fein/ *ad.* 乐意地，欣然地

② painstaking /'peinsteikiŋ/ *n.* 辛苦，工夫

③ hare /hεə/ *n.* 野兔

④ venturous /'ventʃərəs/ *a.* 好冒险的，大胆的

⑤ tortoise /'tɔːtəs/ *n.* 龟

⑥ in proportion to 与……成比例

⑦ domestic /də'mestik/ *n.* 驯养的家畜

⑧ scythe /saið/ *n.* 长柄的大镰刀

⑨ sickle /'sikl/ *n.* 镰刀

I could do was to make one, as well as I could, out of one of the **broadswords**[1], or **cutlasses**[2], which I saved among the arms out of the ship.

When it was growing, and grown, I have observed already how many things I wanted to fence it, secure it, **mow**[3] or reap it, cure and carry it home, **thrash**[4], part it from the **chaff**[5], and save it. Then I wanted a **mill**[6] to **grind**[7] it, **sieves**[8] to **dress**[9] it, **yeast**[10] and salt to make it into bread, and an oven to bake it; but all these things I did without, as shall be observed; and yet the corn was an inestimable comfort and advantage to me too. All this, as I said, made everything laborious and **tedious**[11] to me; but that there was no help for. Neither was my time so much loss to me, because, as I had divided it, a certain part of it was every day appointed to these works; and as I had resolved to use none of the corn for bread till I had a greater quantity by me, I had the next six months to apply myself wholly, by labour and invention, to furnish myself with **utensils**[12] proper for the performing all the operations necessary for making the corn, when I had it, fit for my use.

I had long studied to make, by some means or other, some earthen vessels, which, indeed, I wanted **sorely**[13], but knew not where to come at them. However, considering the heat of the climate, I did not doubt but if I could find out any clay, I might make some pots that might, being dried in the sun, be hard enough and strong enough to bear handling, and to hold anything that was dry, and required to be kept so.

After having laboured hard to find the clay—to dig it, to **temper**[14] it, to bring it home, and work it—I could not make above two large

无奈之下，只好尽我所能把一把腰刀做了改造。这把腰刀是我从船上的武器中保留下来的。

在谷物生长和成熟时，我要做很多事，又要打篱笆保护它，又要收割后晒干，再往家里运送，又要去壳，簸秕糠，最后收藏起来。此刻我又缺少一只石磨来磨它，缺少一只筛子来筛它，制作面包也缺少酵粉和盐，缺少一个用来烘烤的炉子。所有这些我都没有。但是，只要有了粮食，对我来说就是莫大的安慰和便利。当然，这一切使我做起来很吃力，可是没有什么办法。同时，我也没太浪费时间，因为我已经把时间安排得有条有理，每天排出一点时间来做这些事。我下决心要等到有更多粮食的时候再做面包，在此之前我不会在这上面浪费一粒粮食。这样我有 6 个月的时间去尽心尽力制作加工粮食各项工序所需要的各种器皿，等粮食多起来再去使用。

我早就想采用这样或那样的方法来制作一些陶器，我急需这些东西，但不知道怎样做才能成功。然而，考虑到这里的气温如此之高，我毫不怀疑地相信，只要能找到陶土，我一定能做出一些罐子之类的东西，让它们在太阳底下晒到特别坚硬结实的程度，能够承受得起我拿来拿去，能装一些需要保存的干燥的东西。

我常常很费劲地去找陶土，然后把它挖出来，调和好，搬回家里来，把它做成泥缸，结果花了两个月时间才弄出两只非常难看的大陶器，简直

① broadsword *n.* 阔刀，腰刀
② cutlass /ˈkʌtləs/ *n.* 短剑，弯刀
③ mow /mau/ *v.* 割草
④ thrash /θræʃ/ *v.* 使脱粒，打（谷）
⑤ chaff /tʃaːf/ *n.* 谷壳，糠
⑥ mill /mil/ *n.* 磨粉机
⑦ grind /graind/ *v.* 碾，磨碎
⑧ sieve /siv/ *n.* 筛子
⑨ dress /dres/ *v.* 处理，使……表面光洁
⑩ yeast /jiːst/ *n.* 酵母
⑪ tedious /ˈtiːdiəs/ *a.* 沉闷的，单调乏味的
⑫ utensil /ju(ː)ˈtensl/ *n.* 器具
⑬ sorely /ˈsɔːli/ *ad.* 剧烈地，痛苦地
⑭ temper /ˈtempə/ *v.* （把黏土）炼硬

earthen ugly things, I cannot call them jars, in about two months' labour.

Though I miscarried so much in my design for large pots, yet I made several smaller things with better success; such as little round pots, flat dishes, **pitchers**①, and **pipkins**②, and any things my hand turned to; and the heat of the sun baked them quite hard.

My next concern was to get me a stone **mortar**③ to **stamp**④ or beat some corn in; for as to the mill, there was no thought of arriving at that perfection of art with one pair of hands.

Getting a great block of hard wood as big as I had strength to **stir**⑤, I rounded it, and formed it on the outside with my axe and hatchet, and then with the help of fire and infinite labour, made a hollow place in it, as the Indians in Brazil make their **canoes**⑥. After this, I made a great heavy **pestle**⑦ or beater of the wood called the iron-wood; and this I prepared and laid by against I had my next crop of corn, which I proposed to myself to grind, or rather pound into **meal**⑧ to make bread.

My next difficulty was to make a sieve or searce, to dress my meal, and to part it from the **bran**⑨ and the husk; without which I did not see it possible I could have any bread.

All the **remedy**⑩ that I found for this was, that at last I did remember I had, among the seamen's clothes which were saved out of the ship, some neckcloths of **calico**⑪ or **muslin**⑫; and with some pieces of these I made three small sieves proper enough for the work; and thus I made shift for some years.

The baking part was the next thing to be considered, and how I should make bread when I came to have corn.

无法称其为缸。

我设计大缸的计划虽然如此之失败，但我做的那几样小器皿却获得了成功，像小圆罐、盘子、小瓦锅以及其他我用双手随意捏出来的东西，而且太阳把它们晒得非常结实。

我所想做的第二件事，就是要做一个石臼来舂我的粮食，因为我知道，仅凭一双手无法磨出合乎心愿的粮食来。

我找了一块自己勉强能搬得动的大木头，先用斧头把它削得圆圆的，初步有个模样，然后借助火力，费了很大劲才在上面开了个槽，好像巴西印第安人做独木舟一样。完成这些以后，我又用铁树做了一只又大又重的杵。我把这些东西制作好以后，放在一边，准备等收获粮食之后，用它们捣成面粉，来做面包。

我的下一步困难就是，要做一个筛子来过滤面粉，把它与糠皮分开。没有这种工具，我就无法做出面包来。

我忽然想出一种补救的办法，因为最后我想起来了在我从船上搬下来的那些水手的衣服里面，有几条棉布或毛纱制成的围巾。我拿出 3 块来，做了 3 个很小的筛子，总算还能用，就这样勉强应付了几年。

烘烤是其次要考虑的问题。如果我有了粮食之后，我怎样制作面包?

不久之后，我竟然将自己训练成一位很好的面包师，因为我用大米试制成功了一些糕点。

① pitcher /ˈpitʃə/ *n.* 水罐

② pipkin /ˈpipkin/ *n.* 小瓦罐，小汲桶

③ mortar /ˈmɔːtə/ *n.* 臼，研钵

④ stamp /stæmp/ *v.* 压制，跺

⑤ stir /stə/ *v.* 移动，惹起

⑥ canoe /kəˈnu/ *n.* 独木舟，轻舟

⑦ pestle /ˈpestl/ *n.* 杵

⑧ meal /miːl/ *n.* （谷类的）粗粉

⑨ bran /bræn/ *n.* 糠，麸子

⑩ remedy /ˈremidi/ *n.* 药方，治疗法

⑪ calico /ˈkælikəu/ *n.* 白棉布，印花布

⑫ muslin /ˈmʌzlin/ *n.* 平纹细布，薄纱织物

I became in little time a good pastrycook **into the bargain**[1]; for I made myself several cakes and puddings of the rice.

All the while these things were doing, you may be sure my thoughts ran many times upon the prospect of land which I had seen from the other side of the island; and I was not without secret wishes that I were on shore there, fancying that, seeing the mainland, and an inhabited country, I might find some way or other to **convey**[2] myself further, and perhaps at last find some means of escape.

This at length put me upon thinking whether it was not possible to make myself a canoe, or periagua, such as the natives of those climates make, even without tools, or, as I might say, without hands, of the trunk of a great tree.

I felled a **cedar**[3]-tree, and I question much whether Solomon ever had such a one for the building of the Temple of Jerusalem; it was five feet ten inches **diameter**[4] at the lower part next the **stump**[5], and four feet eleven inches diameter at the end of twenty-two feet; after which it lessened for a while, and then parted into branches. It was not without infinite labour that I felled this tree; I was twenty days **hacking**[6] and **hewing**[7] at it at the bottom; I was fourteen more getting the branches and limbs and the vast spreading head cut off, which I hacked and hewed through with axe and hatchet, and inexpressible labour; after this, it cost me a month to shape it and **dub**[8] it to a proportion, and to something like the bottom of a boat, that it might swim upright as it ought to do. It cost me near three months more to clear the inside, and work it out so as to make an exact boat of it; this I did, indeed, without fire, by mere **mallet**[9] and **chisel**[10], and by the **dint**[11] of hard labour, till I had brought it to be a very handsome periagua, and big

① into the bargain 另外，此外

② convey /kən'vei/ v. 运输，转移

③ cedar /'siːdə/ n. 西洋杉，香柏

④ diameter /dai'æmitə/ n. 直径

⑤ stump /stʌmp/ n. 残株

⑥ hack /hæk/ v. 劈，砍

⑦ hew /hju/ v. 砍

⑧ dub /dʌb/ v. 把（铁片、木板等）锤平，刮光

⑨ mallet /'mælit/ n. 木槌，棒

⑩ chisel /'tʃizl/ n. 凿子

⑪ dint /dint/ n. 力量
by dint of 凭……的力量，靠

你可想像在做这些事情的时候，我的思绪有好几次溜到我在岛的那一头所看到的陆地。我确实有一种秘密的想法，希望能在那里登陆，并且幻想着能看到大陆，如果能找到有人烟居住的地方，那我或许可以找到这样或那样的办法继续前进，也许最后能找到逃生的办法。

最后，这使我想到，即使没有工具，或者，也可以说没有人手，能不能用一棵大树的树干给我自己制作一个热带居住的土人所做的那种独木舟呢?

我砍倒了一棵杉树。我怀疑即使是在所罗门制造耶路撒冷圣殿时也没有用过这样大的木材。在靠近树根的地方，它的直径大约为 5 英尺 10 英寸，在 22 英尺长的末端，它的直径是 4 英尺 11 英寸，然后慢慢细下去，分出许多枝叉。砍倒这颗树确实费了我很大的劲，花费了大约 20 天在大树的根部又砍又劈。我又花了 14 天功夫，才很艰难地砍掉了树枝、树干和撑开的巨大的树顶，这都是用我的斧头一点一点砍出来的，经历了难以描述的艰难。接着，我又用了 1 个月时间按一定比例把它刮得初具模型，成了船底的形状，可以浮在水面上。然后，我花了将近 3 个月的功夫把它内部挖空，做得完全像只小船。我做这一步的时候，并没用火烧，只用槌子和凿子很艰难地把它一点点挖空，最后终于做成了一只很象样的独木舟，它的体积足够大，可以容纳 26 个人，所以，它也足够容纳我和我全部的物品。

enough to have carried six-and-twenty men, and consequently big enough to have carried me and all my cargo.

But all my devices to get it into the water failed me; though they cost me infinite labour too.

This grieved me heartily; and now I saw, though too late, the folly of beginning a work before we count the cost, and before we judge rightly of our own strength to go through with it.

I had now been here so long that many things which I had brought on shore for my help were either quite gone, or very much wasted and near spent.

The next thing to my ink being wasted was that of my bread—I mean the biscuit which I brought out of the ship.

My clothes, too, began to decay; so I set to work, tailoring, or rather, indeed, **botching**[①], for I made most **piteous**[②] work of it. However, I made shift to make two or three new **waistcoats**[③], which I hoped would serve me a great while; as for **breeches**[④] or **drawers**[⑤], I made but a very sorry shift indeed till afterwards.

I spent a great deal of time and pains to make an umbrella; I was, indeed, in great want of one, and had a great mind to make one.

I cannot say that after this, for five years, any extraordinary thing happened to me, but I lived on in the same course, in the same **posture**[⑥] and place, as before; the chief things I was employed in, besides my yearly labour of planting my barley and rice, and curing my raisins, of both which I always kept up; I say, besides this yearly labour, and my daily pursuit of going out with my gun, I had one labour, to make a canoe, which at last I finished; so that, by digging a **canal**[⑦] to it of six feet wide and four feet deep, I brought it into the **creek**[⑧], almost half a

然而，尽管我做这项工作历尽千辛万苦，但一切使它下水的努力都失败了。

这件事使我非常伤心，我现在才明白太晚了，开始做一件事之前，如果不考虑代价，不预先对自己的力量有一个正确的估计，实在是太愚蠢了。

因为我来到岛上已经太久了，我带到岛上可用的东西，不是已经用光了，就是差不多要用完了。

我已经用完了墨水，从船上搬到岛上的饼干现在也吃光了。

我的衣服也开始破烂不堪了。于是我又当起了裁缝。我的手艺太差了，与其说是做裁缝，还不如说是瞎缝一气。我还是勉强做成了两三件新背心，看起来还能穿一段时间。至于短裤，我到了后来才做成了一件很不像样的成品。

我又用了不少时间，吃了不少苦头，为自己做了一把伞。我非常需要一把伞，也特别想做一把伞。

我说不清在此后的 5 年中，我的生活境况发生了什么特别的变化。我按以往的方式生活着，在同一个地方居住，都和从前一样。我的主要工作，除了每年照例种我的大麦和稻子、晒我的葡萄干，然后把它们贮存起来，我是说，除了常年的劳作之外，每天还带枪出去打猎。我在一条独木舟上花了很大的功夫，最后还是完成了，并且为此挖了一条小运河，有 6 英尺宽、4 英尺深，把它放到了半英里以外的小河里。至于先前制造

① botch /bɔtʃ/ *v.* 拙笨地修补，糟蹋

② piteous /ˈpitiəs/ *a.* 哀怨的，可怜的

③ waistcoat /ˈweistkəut/ *n.* 背心

④ breech /briːtʃ/ *n.* 短裤

⑤ drawers /ˈdrɔːəz/ *n.* 衬裤

⑥ posture /ˈpɔstʃə/ *n.* 姿势，态度

⑦ canal /kəˈnæl/ *n.* 运河，沟渠

⑧ creek /kriːk/ *n.* 小湾，小溪

mile. As for the first, which was so vastly big, for I made it without considering beforehand, as I ought to have done, how I should be able to launch it, so, never being able to bring it into the water, or bring the water to it, I was obliged to let it lie where it was as a **memorandum**① to teach me to be wiser the next time.

I improved myself in this time in all the mechanic exercises which my necessities put me upon applying myself to; and I believe I should, upon occasion, have made a very good carpenter, especially considering how few tools I had.

I think I was never more vain of my own performance, or more joyful for anything I found out, than for my being able to make a tobacco-pipe.

In my **wicker**②-ware also I improved much, and made abundance of necessary baskets, as well as my invention showed me; though not very handsome, yet they were such as were very handy and convenient for laying things up in, or fetching things home.

But being now in the eleventh year of my residence, and, as I have said, my ammunition growing low, I set myself to study some art to trap and **snare**③ the goats, to see whether I could not catch some of them alive.

So I dug several large pits in the earth, in places where I had observed the goats used to feed, and over those pits I placed **hurdles**④ of my own making too, with a great weight upon them.

Going one morning to see my traps, I found in one of them a large old he-goat; and in one of the others three kids, a male and two females.

As to the old one, I knew not what to do with him; he was so

的独木舟，实在太大了，由于事先考虑不周，我本来应该考虑到的，没有考虑到如何把它放到水里去，我不能将独木舟拖到水里，也无法把水引到它的下面来，只好让它躺在那里作个记念，提醒我下次聪明点。

① memorandum /ˌmeməˈrændəm/ *n.* 备忘录

在此期间，由于生活所迫，逼着我自己去适应，我在各种技术上都有一些进步。我相信，如果有机会，我有可能成为一个很不错的木匠，尤其要考虑到我手头并没几样工具。

我认为，在我的各项成就中，最让我高兴，最让我引以自豪的是，我竟然做出来一只烟斗。

我在编制藤器方面也有不小的进步，我编了大量的有用处的篮子，并且凝聚了我的全部匠心。尽管这些篮子不大好看，然而使用起来却很方便适用，无论是放东西还是带东西回家都是如此。

② wicker /ˈwikə/ *n.* 藤条，柳条

现在我来到岛上已经是第 11 个年头了。正如我所说的那样，我的弹药越来越少了，于是我开始琢磨如何用陷阱来捕羊，看看能不能活捉上一两只。

③ snare /snɛə/ *v.* 以陷阱捕获

于是，我在我观察到的山羊常吃草的地方，在地上挖了几个大陷阱，然后在陷井上盖了几块自己做的木格子，再压上一些重物。

④ hurdle /ˈhəːdl/ *n.* 障碍

一天早上，我前去看陷阱，只见一个陷阱里有 1 只老公羊，另一个陷阱里有 3 只小山羊，其中 1 只是公的，两只是母的。

我不知道怎么对付那只老公羊，因为它很凶，我几乎不敢下到陷阱里接近它。也就是说，我不

fierce I **durst**[①] not go into the pit to him; that is to say, to bring him away alive, which was what I wanted.

For the present I let him go, knowing no better at that time; then I went to the three kids, and taking them one by one, I tied them with strings together, and with some difficulty brought them all home.

It was a good while before they would feed; but throwing them some sweet corn, it tempted them, and they began to be tame.

But then it occurred to me that I must keep the tame from the wild, or else they would always run wild when they grew up; and the only way for this was to have some enclosed piece of ground, well fenced either with **hedge**[②] or **pale**[③], to keep them in so effectually, that those within might not break out, or those without break in.

This was a great undertaking for one pair of hands yet, as I saw there was an absolute necessity for doing it, my first work was to find out a proper piece of ground, where there was likely to be **herbage**[④] for them to eat, water for them to drink, and cover to keep them from the sun.

I was about three months hedging in the first piece.

This answered my end, and in about a year and a half I had a flock of about twelve goats, kids and all; and in two years more I had forty-three, besides several that I took and killed for my food. After that, I enclosed five several pieces of ground to feed them in, with little **pens**[⑤] to drive them into, to take them as I wanted, and gates out of one piece of ground into another.

But this was not all; for now I not only had goat's flesh to feed on when I pleased, but milk too—a thing which, indeed, in the beginning, I did not so much as think of.

① durst /dəːst/ ［古］dare的过去式

敢按照自己的想法把它活捉出来。

当时，我想不出更好的办法，只好把它放走了。然后我就走到那些小山羊旁边，把它们一只一只捉出来，用细绳把它们拴在一起，费了很大周折才把它们带回家。

3 只山羊起初不肯吃东西，我丢给它们一些新鲜的玉米，吊吊它们的胃口，最后它们被驯服了。

这时候，我忽然想到，我必须把驯养的羊和野羊隔离开，不然它们一长大，肯定会跑掉的。唯一有效的办法，就是找一个四周封闭的地方，扎上牢固的篱笆和木栅，把这些羊圈在里面，使里边的不至于冲出去，外边的不至于冲进来。

② hedge /hedʒ/ *n.* 树篱

③ pale /peil/ *n.* 尖木桩

对于一个没有什么工具的人来说，这其实是一项大工程，也是一件绝对必要的事情，因此我第一件要做的事是要物色一块好地，在那儿这些山羊有草吃、有水喝并且可以遮荫的地方。

④ herbage /ˈhəːbidʒ/ *n.* 草本，草

我用了几乎 3 个月，圈好了第一块地。

我的目标总算实现了。在近一年半的时间里，我已拥有了大小山羊一共 12 只。又过了两年，不算我已经宰杀吃掉的几只，我已有 43 只羊了。在那之后，我又圈了五六块地方来喂养山羊，把羊赶到许多小羊圈中，在各个圈地之间有门相通，我随时可以去捕捉它们。

⑤ pen /pen/ *n.*（家畜的）栏，圈

但是这并不是全部，我现在不仅随时有新鲜的羊肉吃，还有羊奶喝。这是我过去做梦都想不到的事情。

我已经建立起了自己的奶房，有时候一天可

For now I set up my dairy, and had sometimes a **gallon**① or two of milk in a day. And as Nature, who gives supplies of food to every creature, **dictates**② even naturally how to make use of it, so I, that had never milked a cow, much less a goat, or seen butter or cheese made only when I was a boy, after a great many **essays**③ and **miscarriages**④, made both butter and cheese at last.

Then, to see how like a king I dined, too, all alone, attended by my servants! Poll, as if he had been my favourite, was the only person permitted to talk to me. My dog, who was now grown old and crazy, and had found no **species**⑤ to multiply his kind upon, sat always at my right hand; and two cats, one on one side of the table and one on the other, expecting now and then a bit from my hand, as a mark of especial favour.

But now I come to a new scene of my life. It happened one day, about noon, going towards my boat, I was exceedingly surprised with the print of a man's naked foot on the shore, which was very plain to be seen on the sand. I stood like one thunderstruck, or as if I had seen an **apparition**⑥. I listened, I looked round me, but I could hear nothing, nor see anything; I went up to a rising ground to look farther; I went up the shore and down the shore, but it was all one; I could see no other impression but that one. I went to it again to see if there were any more, and to observe if it might not be my fancy; but there was no room for that, for there was exactly the print of a foot—toes, heel, and every part of a foot. How it came thither I knew not, nor could I in the least imagine; but after innumerable **fluttering**⑦ thoughts, like a man perfectly confused and out of myself, I came home to my fortification, not feeling, as we say, the ground I went on, but terrified to the last

以挤出一两加仑①羊奶。大自然不仅为每个生物提供食物，同时也指导②它们如何自然而然地去加以利用。我本人从来没有挤过牛奶，更没有挤过羊奶，只在小时候看过别人制作奶油和奶酪，但经过多次的试验③，终于做成了奶油和奶酪。

你看我用餐的时候，俨然像位国王，并不感到孤单。一个人高高坐在上面，臣仆们在旁侍候着我。波儿就是我的宠臣，只有它才有权利与我交谈。我那条没法找到同类配对繁衍的狗，现在又老又昏聩，总是坐在我的右侧。那两只猫呢？一只坐在桌子一边，一只坐在桌子另一边，常常希望能从我的手中得到些特殊的赏赐。

不料，我的生活现在又发生了新变化。大约是一天中午，我正准备去看我的船，忽然发现一个人的赤脚脚印，清清楚楚地印在沙滩上。这简直把我吓坏了。我呆呆地站在那里，像挨了一个晴天霹雳或是见到了鬼魂一样。我侧耳听听，又回头四周看看，可是什么也看不见，什么也听不见。我跑上一个高坡往远处眺望，又在海边来回跑了几次，可是毫无收获。除了这个脚印外，我再也找不到其他脚印。我走到这个脚印跟前，看看还有没有别的脚印，是不是我个人的幻觉，可是完全不是那么回事，因为这的确是一个人的脚印，脚趾头，脚后跟，样样俱全。至于这个脚印是如何来的，我无从猜测。我像一个神经失常、不能控制住自己的人一样，在那里胡思乱想了一气，然后像一阵风似的抬脚拼命往我的家跑，跑回了我的防御工事。我内心慌乱极了，每走两三

① gallon /ˈgælən/ *n.* 加仑

② dictate /dikˈteit/ *v.* 指令，指示

③ essay /ˈesei/ *n.* 尝试，试验

④ miscarriage /misˈkæridʒ/ *n.* 流产，失败

⑤ species /ˈspiːʃiz/ *n.* 物种，种类

⑥ apparition /ˌæpəˈriʃən/ *n.* 鬼，幽灵

⑦ flutter /ˈflʌtə/ *v.* 摆动，烦扰

degree, looking behind me at every two or three steps, mistaking every bush and tree, and fancying every stump at a distance to be a man. Nor is it possible to describe how many various shapes my **affrighted**[①] imagination represented things to me in, how many wild ideas were found every moment in my fancy, and what strange, unaccountable **whimsies**[②] came into my thoughts by the way.

When I came to my castle, for so I think I called it ever after this, I fled into it like one pursued. Whether I went over by the ladder, as first **contrived**[③], or went in at the hole in the rock, which I had called a door, I cannot remember.

I slept none that night; the farther I was from the occasion of my fright, the greater my apprehensions were, which is something contrary to the nature of such things, and especially to the usual practice of all creatures in fear; but I was so embarrassed with my own frightful ideas of the thing, that I formed nothing but **dismal**[④] imaginations to myself, even though I was now a great way off.

In the middle of these **cogitations**[⑤], apprehensions, and reflections, it came into my thoughts one day that all this might be a mere **chimera**[⑥] of my own, and that this foot might be the print of my own foot, when I came on shore from my boat: this cheered me up a little, too, and I began to persuade myself it was all a **delusion**[⑦]; that it was nothing else but my own foot; and why might I not come that way from the boat, as well as I was going that way to the boat?

Now I began to take courage, and to **peep**[⑧] abroad again, for I had not stirred out of my castle for three days and nights, so that I began to starve for provisions; for I had little or nothing within doors but some barley-cakes and water.

步就要回头去看一看，连远处的小树丛、枯树枝都误以为是个人了。我自己一路上所受到的惊吓，在我脑海中产生了各种各样的幻觉，在我的幻觉中又出现了不少荒诞不经的想法，这些想法每时每刻都夹杂了一些稀奇古怪的妄想，那简直不知道该怎么描绘。

我一口气跑回我的城堡，我想以后就得这么称呼它了。我惟恐后面有人追赶，立刻钻了进去。至于我是爬梯子进了岩洞还是从所谓的门爬进来，我已经记不清了。

我一整夜都没合眼。离受惊吓的时间越远，我的恐惧反而越大。这种情形似乎不合常理，尤其是与处于恐惧心理状态的一般生物的常理不一样。其实，我不断用一种大惊小怪的想法吓唬自己，因此专门往坏处想，尽管离这件事越来越远。

我这样疑神疑鬼、焦虑不安地过了一段时间后，突然有一天，我想这一切也许是我个人的幻觉吧，那脚印也许是我从船上下来登陆时自己留下的。这么一想，我的精神又为之一振，并且开始努力使自己相信，这一切都是我个人的幻觉，那只不过是我自己的脚印，并没有什么了不起的事。我想，我能在那个地方上船，为什么就不能在那个地方下船呢？

因此，我的胆子又大了起来，想出去窥探一下。我已经三天三夜没有出城堡了，开始面临供应不足的问题，家中除了一些大麦饼和水之外，几乎没有什么可吃的东西了。

于是，我就大着胆子，努力让自己相信那只

① affrighte /ə'frait/ *v.* ［古］恐吓，恐惧

② whimsy /'(h)wimzi/ *n.* 怪念头，心情浮动

③ contrive /kən'traiv/ *v.* 设计，图谋

④ dismal /'dizməl/ *a.* 阴沉的，凄凉的

⑤ cogitation /ˌkɔdʒi'teiʃən/ *n.* 思考，苦思

⑥ chimera /kai'miərə/ *n.* 梦幻

⑦ delusion /di'luːʒən/ *n.* 错觉

⑧ peep /piːp/ *v.* 窥视

Encouraging myself, therefore, with the belief that this was nothing but the print of one of my own feet, and that I might be truly said to start at my own shadow, I began to go abroad again, and went to my country house to milk my flock.

But I could not persuade myself fully of this till I should go down to the shore again, and see this print of a foot, and measure it by my own, and see if there was any **similitude**① or fitness, that I might be assured it was my own foot: but when I came to the place, first, it appeared evidently to me, that when I laid up my boat I could not possibly be on shore anywhere thereabouts; secondly, when I came to measure the mark with my own foot, I found my foot not so large by a great deal. Both these things filled my head with new imaginations, and gave me the **vapours**② again to the highest degree, so that I shook with cold like one in an **ague**③; and I went home again, filled with the belief that some man or men had been on shore there; or, in short, that the island was inhabited, and I might be surprised before I was aware; and what course to take for my security I knew not.

This confusion of my thoughts kept me awake all night; but in the morning I fell asleep; and having, by the amusement of my mind, been as it were tired, and my spirits exhausted, I slept very soundly, and waked much better **composed**④ than I had ever been before. And now I began to think **sedately**⑤.

Now, I began sorely to repent that I had dug my cave so large as to bring a door through again, which door, as I said, came out beyond where my fortification joined to the rock; upon **maturely**⑥ considering this, therefore, I resolved to draw me a second fortification, in the same manner of a semicircle, at a distance from my wall, just where I

不过是我个人留的脚印，相信我是在吓唬自己。就这样，我又开始走出去，又回到我自己的房子，跑去挤羊奶了。

但是，我心里还是有点疑惑，不能完全说服自己相信这一点，除非我再到海边去一趟，去亲自看看那个脚印，并且用自己的脚与沙滩上的那个脚印比一比，看一看是不是一样大小，这样我才会确信那是我自己的脚印。可是我一到了那边就发现，当初我放小船的时候，很显然，我决不可能在那个地方附近上岸，这是第一点；第二点，当我用自己的脚和那个脚印相比较时，我的脚明显要比那个脚印小。这使我头脑又处于新的混乱状态，我全身直打冷战，就像一个得了疟病的人一样。我再次回到家里，深信有人在那里曾上过岸，简单说来，就是岛屿上已经有人了，说不定什么时候要对我来一次袭击，而我不知道要采取什么措施来保障自己的安全。

我就这样胡思乱想了整个晚上，一直到第二天早晨才昏昏睡去。由于这些可笑的念头使我用脑过度，精疲力竭，晚上我睡得很沉。我醒来之后，感到内心比任何时候都平静。现在我开始冷静思考目前所遇到的问题了。

我现在又开始非常后悔，我把我的山洞挖得太大了，而且在围墙和岩石连接的地方又开了个门，就是我曾经提到的那个门。因此，对这些事情经过全盘考虑之后，我决定在围墙外边，也就是在 12 年前种了两行树的地方（我曾经提到过这些），再以同样的方式为我筑起一道壁垒——

① similitude /si'militjuːd/ *n.* 比喻，相似

② vapour /'veipə/ *n.* 空想，幻想

③ ague /'eigju/*n.* 疟疾，打冷颤

④ composed /kəm'pəuzd/ *a.* 镇静的，沉着的

⑤ sedately /si 'deitli/ *ad.* 镇静地，安详地

⑥ maturely /mə'tjuəli/ *ad.* 成熟地，充分地

had planted a double row of trees about twelve years before, of which I made mention.

While this was doing, I was not altogether careless of my other affairs; for I had a great concern upon me for my little herd of goats; they were not only a ready supply to me on every occasion, and began to be sufficient for me, without the expense of powder and shot, but also without the **fatigue**① of hunting after the wild ones.

Accordingly, I spent some time to find out the most retired parts of the island; and I pitched upon one, which was as private, indeed, as my heart could wish: it was a little **damp**② piece of ground in the middle of the hollow and thick woods, where, as is observed, I almost lost myself once before, endeavouring to come back that way from the eastern part of the island. Here I found a clear piece of land, near three acres, so surrounded with woods that it was almost an **enclosure**③ by nature; at least, it did not want near so much labour to make it so as the other piece of ground I had worked so hard at.

After I had thus secured one part of my little living stock, I went about the whole island, searching for another private place to make such another **deposit**④; when, wandering more to the west point of the island than I had ever done yet, and looking out to sea, I thought I saw a boat upon the sea, at a great distance. I had found a **perspective**⑤ glass or two in one of the seamen's chests, which I saved out of our ship, but I had it not about me; and this was so remote that I could not tell what to make of it, though I looked at it till my eyes were not able to hold to look any longer; whether it was a boat or not I do not know, but as I **descended**⑥ from the hill I could see no more of it, so I gave it over; only I resolved to go no more out without a perspective

一道半圆形的壁垒。

我一方面做着这项工作，另一方面也没有忽略别的事情。我还有许多事情要去关心，我很在意我那数量不多的羊群。这些羊不仅可以随时供我食用，而且足以够我享受，使我节省了大量的火药和子弹，还使我不必费力去追捕那些野山羊。

于是，我花了点儿时间，去寻找这个岛屿上最偏僻之处。我选定了一个异常幽静的地方，非常符合我心意。这是一块小小的低湿地块，正处于一片茂密的森林中间。这片森林也就是我过去从这座岛屿东部回来，几乎要迷路的地方。在这片低湿地块中，我找到了一块没有树木的平地，大约有 3 英亩大，四周有树木环绕，几乎像一块天然的圈地，至少不需要花费太多的精力去圈它，不像我圈别的地方一样。

我把我的少得可怜的一部分家畜安置妥当之后，打算在整个岛屿寻找另外一块偏僻的地方，想再建立起一座类似的仓库。未曾预料到，当我走到岛屿的最西角时，我朝海里一望，仿佛看见远处海面上有一艘船在航行。我原来从那艘我们逃生的破船上一个船员的箱子里找到过一两副望远镜，可是现在我没有带在身边。这艘船离我如此遥远，我简直看不清楚是什么东西在海面上，尽管我看得眼睛都痛了。那个东西究竟是不是一艘船，我不知道。当我从山上下来时，它已经不见了，也只好随它去了。不过我下决心，以后出门时一定要带一副望远镜。

① fatigue /fə'tiːg/ *n.* 疲乏，疲劳

② damp /dæmp/ *a.* 潮湿的

③ enclosure /in'kləuʒə/ *n.* 围墙，圈地

④ deposit /di'pɔzit/ *n.* 储蓄，贮存

⑤ perspective /pə'spektiv/ *n.* 透镜，望远镜

⑥ descend /di'send/ *v.* 降，下

glass in my pocket.

When I was come down the hill to the shore, as I said above, being the SW. point of the island, I was perfectly **confounded**[①] and amazed; nor is it possible for me to express the horror of my mind at seeing the shore spread with skulls, hands, feet, and other bones of human bodies; and particularly I observed a place where there had been a fire made, and a circle dug in the earth, like a **cockpit**[②], where I supposed the savage wretches had sat down to their human feastings upon the bodies of their fellow-creatures.

My stomach grew sick, and I was just at the point of fainting, when nature discharged the disorder from my stomach; and having **vomited**[③] with uncommon violence, I was a little relieved, but could not bear to stay in the place a moment; so I got up the hill again with all the speed I could, and walked on towards my own habitation.

When I came a little out of that part of the island I stood still awhile, as amazed.

My invention now ran quite another way; for night and day I could think of nothing but how I might destroy some of the monsters in their cruel, bloody entertainment, and if possible save the victim they should bring hither to destroy. It would take up a larger volume than this whole work is intended to be to set down all the contrivances I **hatched**[④], or rather **brooded**[⑤] upon, in my thoughts, for the destroying these creatures, or at least frightening them so as to prevent their coming hither any more.

After I had thus laid the scheme of my design, and in my imagination put it in practice, I continually made my tour every morning to the top of the hill, which was from my castle, as I called it,

我从小山上下来，来到了岛屿的西南角后，走到了上面我提到的那块沙滩，立刻被吓得目瞪口呆，我不知道如何形容我心中那份恐惧，我看见海岸上到处都是人的头骨、手骨、脚骨以及人体上其他的骨头。特别要说的是，我又发现地上有一个斗鸡场似的圆圈，曾经生过火，我猜想大概是那些野蛮人曾经围坐在那里，用同类的肉体举办过残忍的宴会。

我觉得肠胃异常难受，而且几乎要晕倒了，最终要把胃里的东西都翻出来。经过一阵排山倒海般的呕吐，我才觉得多少好受了点，但我一分钟也不想停留在这个鬼地方，于是我飞也似的又跑上那座小山（尽我最快的速度），冲向我自己的住处。

尽管离开海岸已有一段路，但我还是惊魂不定，在路上停留了好半天。

我现在把创造发明的心思用到了其他地方了，整日整夜老是在想如何乘那伙野蛮人在举行那种残忍、血腥的宴会时杀掉他们几个，而且如有可能，救出他们将要杀害的牺牲品。要把我的全部计划记下来，得写一本比这本更厚的书，我必须采取一些措施，希望能消灭那些野蛮人，或者至少吓唬一下他们，叫他们再也不敢到岛上来。

当我制订好我的计划，并且想把自己设想的计划付诸实施以后，我每天早上都要跑到远离我的“城堡”（我就这样称呼它）大约 3 英里地的小山头上去巡逻，看看海上有没有小船驶近岛

① confound /kən'faund/ *v.* 使混淆，使狼狈

② cockpit /'kɔkpit/ *n.* 斗鸡场

③ vomit /'vɔmit/ *v.* 吐出，呕吐

④ hatch /hætʃ/ *v.* 孵，孵出

⑤ brood /bruːd/ *v.* 孵，沉思

about three miles or more, to see if I could observe any boats upon the sea, coming near the island, or standing over towards it.

As long as I kept my daily tour to the hill, to look out, so long also I kept up the **vigour**① of my design, and my spirits seemed to be all the while in a suitable frame for so outrageous an **execution**② as the killing twenty or thirty naked savages.

But this was by the bye. While I was cutting down some wood here, I perceived that, behind a very thick branch of low brushwood or underwood, there was a kind of hollow place. I was curious to look in it; and getting with difficulty into the mouth of it, I found it was pretty large, that is to say, sufficient for me to stand upright in it, and perhaps another with me; but I must confess to you that I made more haste out than I did in, when looking farther into the place, and which was perfectly dark, I saw two broad shining eyes of some creature, whether devil or man I knew not, which **twinkled**③ like two stars; the **dim**④ light from the cave's mouth shining directly in, and making the reflection. However, after some pause I recovered myself, and began to call myself a thousand fools, and to think that he that was afraid to see the devil was not fit to live twenty years in an island all alone; and that I might well think there was nothing in this cave that was more frightful than myself. Upon this, **plucking**⑤ up my courage, I took up a firebrand, and in I rushed again, with the stick flaming in my hand. I had not gone three steps in before I was almost as frightened as before; for I heard a very loud sigh, like that of a man in some pain, and it was followed by a broken noise, as of words half expressed, and then a deep sigh again. I stepped back, and was indeed struck with such a surprise that it put me into a cold sweat, and if I had had a hat on my

屿，或者有没有小船在它的近处停泊。

在我天天到小山上巡视和观望的时候，我始终精神饱满，保持着实施我自己那份计划的干劲，似乎随时都可以做出惊天动地的举措，把那二三十个赤身裸体的野人一口气杀掉。

① vigour /ˈvigə/ *n.* 精力

② execution /ˌeksiˈkjuːʃən/ *n.* 实行，执行；处死

这些事情暂且不提。有一天，我正在这里伐树木，突然看见在一片浓密的矮丛林后面，好像有一个深坑。我非常好奇地想钻进去看看。我很吃劲地费了许多功夫，才钻进坑口，发现里面非常大，也就是说，我在里面站直了还绰绰有余，甚至还可以再容纳一个人进来。不过老实说，我钻进去的时候尽管不慢，但逃出来的时候更快，因为我朝一片漆黑的洞里望去，忽然看见有两只发光的眼睛，在从洞口射进去的微弱的光线的反射下，像两颗星星在闪耀，不知是魔鬼的还是人的眼睛。尽管如此，片刻之后，我又镇静下来，连声骂自己是个糊涂虫，并且心里想，一个害怕鬼怪的人本身就不配独自一个人在岛上居住20年，而且我确信，在这个山洞里，还有什么东西比我更可怕的呢？于是，我又鼓足了勇气，手里举了一根点燃了的大火把，重新钻了进去。我刚走了几步，我几乎又像上回一样吓了一跳，因为我忽然听见一种好像一个人在痛苦中发出的叹息声，接着又是一阵阵断断续续的声音，好像人在半吞半吐的说话，然后又是一声深深的叹息。我立刻往后退了几步，真的大吃一惊，出了一身冷汗，要是我的脑袋上戴着一顶帽子，我那堆竖起

③ twinkle /ˈtwiŋkl/ *v.* 闪烁，使……闪耀

④ dim /dim/ *adj.* 暗淡的，模糊的

⑤ pluck /plʌk/ *v.* 摘，拔
pluck up 鼓起勇气

head, I will not answer for it that my hair might not have lifted it off. But still plucking up my spirits as well as I could, and encouraging myself a little with considering that the power and presence of God was everywhere, and was able to protect me, I stepped forward again, and by the light of the firebrand, holding it up a little over my head, I saw lying on the ground a **monstrous**①, frightful old he-goat, just making his will, as we say, and **gasping**② for life, and, dying, indeed, of mere old age. I stirred him a little to see if I could get him out, and he essayed to get up, but was not able to raise himself.

I was now recovered from my surprise, and began to look round me.

The place I was in was a most delightful **cavity**③, or **grotto**④, though perfectly dark; the floor was dry and level, and had a sort of a small loose **gravel**⑤ upon it, so that there was no **nauseous**⑥ or **venomous**⑦ creature to be seen, neither was there any damp or wet on the sides or roof. The only difficulty in it was the entrance—which, however, as it was a place of security, and such a **retreat**⑧ as I wanted; I thought was a convenience; so that I was really rejoiced at the discovery, and resolved, without any delay, to bring some of those things which I was most anxious about to this place; particularly, I resolved to bring hither my **magazine**⑨ of powder, and all my spare arms—viz. two fowling-pieces—for I had three in all, and three muskets—for of them I had eight in all.

I was now in the twenty-third year of my residence in this island, and was so naturalised to the place and the manner of living.

I had taught my Poll, as I noted before, to speak; and he did it so

来的头发，说不定就会把它顶起来。但是，我想到手中有枪，想到我那万能的上帝法力无边，无时无刻、随时随地都在保护着我，我便鼓足了勇气，把火把高高地举起来，往前走了几步，借着高举在我头顶上的火把的火光一看，我发现原来地上躺着一只硕大无比的公山羊，就像我们所说，可能是由于老的缘故，几乎快要死了，临死之前发出了喘息声。我推了推那只公山羊，看看能否把它轰出去。它也想站起来，可就是爬不起来。

此刻，我从慌乱中摆脱了出来，开始察看四周的情况。

我现在来到的这个地方，尽管里面黑乎乎的，没有一点光线，但是这个洞穴是那种最美观的洞穴，我感到特别兴奋。洞穴地面又干燥又平坦，上面铺着一层细沙，里面也看不到什么令人恶心的小虫、毒蛇之类的东西，里面也不潮湿。这个洞穴唯一的缺点就是这个洞穴的入口，但是，我觉得，这个洞穴入口的缺陷对我自己极为有利，因为我本身需要一个安全的保障。因此，对这个发现异常高兴，没有丝毫的停顿，立刻马不停蹄地把我最不放心的一部分东西搬了过来，特别是，我下决心把我的火药，多余的枪枝，其中包括两枝鸟枪（我一共有 3 支鸟枪），3 支短枪（我总共有 8 支短枪）。

现在我在这个岛屿上已经住了 23 年了，而且对这个地方、这种生活方式已经习以为常了。

我已经教会了我的波儿说话（波儿就是我以前提到的那只鹦鹉）。它说话如此熟练，如此清

① monstrous /'mɔnstrəs/ *a.* 巨大的，畸形的

② gasp /gaːsp/ *v.* 喘气，喘息

③ cavity /'kæviti/ *n.* 洞，空穴

④ grotto /'grɔtəu/ *n.* 洞穴，岩穴

⑤ gravel /'grævəl/ *n.* 碎石

⑥ nauseous /'nɔːsjəs/ *a.* 令人作呕的

⑦ venomous /'venəməs/ *a.* 恶意的，有毒的

⑧ retreat /ri'triːt/ *n.* 休息寓所，隐居地

⑨ magazine /ˌmægə'ziːn/ *n.* 仓库，军火库

familiarly, and talked so **articulately**[1] and plain, that it was very pleasant to me; and he lived with me no less than six-and-twenty years. My dog was a pleasant and loving companion to me for no less than sixteen years of my time, and then died of mere old age. As for my cats, they **multiplied**[2], as I have observed, to that degree that I was obliged to shoot several of them at first, to keep them from devouring me and all I had; but at length, when the two old ones I brought with me were gone, and after some time continually driving them from me, and letting them have no provision with me, they all ran wild into the woods, except two or three favourites, which I kept tame. Besides these I always kept two or three household kids about me, whom I taught to feed out of my hand; and I had two more parrots, which talked pretty well, and would all call "Robin Crusoe," but none like my first; nor, indeed, did I take the pains with any of them that I had done with him. I had also several tame sea-fowls, whose name I knew not, that I caught upon the shore, and cut their wings.

It was now the month of December, as I said above, in my twenty-third year; and this, being the southern **solstice**[3], for winter I cannot call it, was the particular time of my harvest, and required me to be pretty much abroad in the fields, when, going out early in the morning, even before it was thorough daylight. I was surprised with seeing a light of some fire upon the shore, at a distance from me of about two miles, toward that part of the island where I had observed some savages had been, as before.

I was indeed terribly surprised at the sight, and stopped short within my grove, not daring to go out, **lest**[4] I might be surprised; and yet I had no more peace within, from the apprehensions I had that if

① articulately /aːˈtikjulitli/ *ad.* 发音清晰地

② multiply /ˈmʌltiplai/ *v.* 繁殖

③ solstice /ˈsɔlstis/ *n.* 至，至点，至日

④ lest /lest /*conj.* 惟恐，以免

楚，真让人高兴。它与我一起生活了不止26年。我的狗，也是一位非常有趣而活泼可爱的伴侣，与我共同生活了不少于16年，直到它老迈而死。至于我的那些猫，它们繁殖得实在太多了，我开始的时候不得不开枪打死其中的几只，免得它们把我所有的东西都吃光。后来，我带来的那两只猫死了，我又不断驱赶那些小猫，不肯给他们吃东西，结果它们都跑到了树林里变成了野猫，只有我所钟爱的两三只小猫，被我驯养在家里。此外，我还在身边养了两三只小山羊，教会它们在我这里吃东西。我养的两只鹦鹉，话也说的不错，也都会叫“鲁宾逊”，却远比不上第一只。当然，我在它们身上投入的精力也不及第一只鹦鹉多。我养了几只海鸟，也不晓得叫什么名字，是在海边捉住，剪短了它们的翅膀喂养起来的。

现在已经是我来到岛上第23年的12月，正是冬至前后，但我不称之为冬季，因为这正是我收获的特殊季节。我一个人必须天天要出门，早上很早起床赶到田地里去，甚至天还没有完全大亮。有一天大清早，我忽然看见远处海岸上有一片火光，距我大约两英里远，也就是在我发现野人足迹的那个方向。

见到这种景象，我确实被吓坏了，便在小树林里停了下来，不敢再往外走，害怕受到突然袭击，至少被吓得有点胆颤心惊。我的心此刻再也平静不下来了，我担心，如果这些野人在岛上走来走去，看见我那些已经收割和尚未收割的庄

these savages, in rambling over the island, should find my corn standing or cut, or any of my works or improvements, they would immediately conclude that there were people in the place, and would then never rest till they had found me out. In this extremity I went back directly to my castle, pulled up the ladder after me, and made all things without look as wild and natural as I could.

Then I prepared myself within, putting myself in a posture of defence. I continued in this posture about two hours, and began to be impatient for **intelligence**① abroad, for I had no spies to send out. After sitting a while longer, and musing what I should do in this case, I was not able to bear sitting in **ignorance**② longer; so setting up my ladder to the side of the hill, where there was a flat place, as I observed before, and then pulling the ladder after me, I set it up again and mounted the top of the hill, and pulling out my perspective glass, which I had taken on purpose, I laid me down flat on my belly on the ground, and began to look for the place. I presently found there were no less than nine naked savages sitting round a small fire they had made, not to warm them, for they had no need of that, the weather being extremely hot, but, as I supposed, to dress some of their **barbarous**③ diet of human flesh which they had brought with them, whether alive or dead I could not tell.

They had two canoes with them, which they had **hauled**④ up upon the shore; and as it was then **ebb**⑤ of tide, they seemed to me to wait for the return of the flood to go away again.

As I expected, so it proved; for as soon as the tide made to the westward I saw them all take boat and row (or **paddle**⑥ as we call it) away.

稼，看见我的某些建筑物，他们一定会猜到这座岛屿上有人，他们非把我搜出来不可。想到这些，我立刻跑回我的城堡，把梯子收起来，并把外面一切东西尽可能安排成荒芜而自然的样子。

然后我又在内部做好准备，采取防范措施。我在这种状态下呆了大约两小时，就开始急于想知道外面的信息，可我派不出去什么侦探去打听消息。我又在家里多坐了一会儿，考虑自己如何应付当前出现的这种情况。最后，我觉得无法再这样耐着性子坐在家里等候下去，于是就把梯子搭在山岩旁边，登上了前面讲过的一段小土坡，随后又把梯子抽上来放在小土坡上，爬上了山顶。我平卧在山顶上，拿起我特意带在身边的望远镜，开始向那一带地方望去。我立刻发现那边有不少于 9 个赤身裸体的野人，他们正围坐在火堆边。这显然不是在取暖，因为现在天气这么热，根本用不着取暖。根据我的猜测，他们大概是在举办人肉宴席，至于他们带来的被烹调的究竟是死人还是活人，我就说不清了。

他们总共来了两条独木舟，已经被拉到了岸上。此时正是退潮的时候，他们可能要等到潮水来的时候才走。

果然不出我的所料（事实证明了一切），当潮水开始往西流的时候，我看见他们就一齐上了船，摇桨而去。

一看见他们上了船划走了，我便背了两枝枪，腰上别了两把信号枪，又取了一把没有鞘的大刀

① intelligence /in'telidʒəns/ *n.* 情报，情报工作

② ignorance /'ignərəns/ *n.* 无知

③ barbarous /'baːbərəs/ *a.* 野蛮的

④ haul /hɔːl/ *v.* 拖

⑤ ebb /eb/ *n.* 退潮

⑥ paddle /'pædl/ *v.* 划桨，戏水

As soon as I saw them shipped and gone, I took two guns upon my shoulders, and two pistols in my **girdle**①, and my great sword by my side without a **scabbard**②, and with all the speed I was able to make went away to the hill.

This was a dreadful sight to me, especially as, going down to the shore, I could see the marks of horror which the dismal work they had been about had left behind it—viz. the blood, the bones, and part of the flesh of human bodies eaten and devoured by those wretches with merriment and sport.

I spent my days now in great **perplexity**③ and anxiety of mind, expecting that I should one day or other fall into the hands of these merciless creatures; and if I did at any time venture abroad, it was not without looking around me with the greatest care and caution imaginable.

The **perturbation**④ of my mind during this fifteen or sixteen months' interval was very great; I slept unquietly, dreamed always frightful dreams, and often started out of my sleep in the night.

It was in the middle of May, on the sixteenth day, I think, as well as my poor wooden calendar would reckon, for I marked all upon the post still; I say, it was on the sixteenth of May that it blew a very great storm of wind all day, with a great deal of lightning and thunder, and; a very **foul**⑤ night it was after it. I knew not what was the particular occasion of it, but as I was reading in the Bible, and taken up with very serious thoughts about my present condition, I was surprised with the noise of a gun, as I thought, fired at sea. I started up in the greatest haste imaginable; and, in a **trice**⑥, **clapped**⑦ my ladder to the middle place of the rock, and pulled it after me; and mounting it the second

挂在腰上，尽我最快的速度向山上跑去。

① girdle /ˈgəːdl/ *n.* 腰带

② scabbard /ˈskæbəd/ *n.* (刀、剑) 鞘

对我来说，这真是一场极为恐怖的景象。更为可怕的是，当我走到海边的时候，我又看见这帮野蛮人走后留下来的惨不忍睹的场面：又是血，又是骨头，又是一块一块的人肉。这些都是那帮野人混蛋享乐时留下的“杰作”。

我现在每天都是在疑惑和焦急中度过，脑子里一直担心自己也会有这么一天，落到这帮毫无人性的畜生手里。我现在偶然大胆外出，也是极其小心翼翼地东瞧瞧西望望。

③ perplexity /pəˈpleksiti/ *n.* 困惑，混乱

在这 15 个月或 16 个月之内，我一直感到自己内心焦躁不安，忧心忡忡。我总是睡不着觉，老是做一些恶梦，并且我晚上经常从梦中惊醒。

④ perturbation /ˌpəːtəːˈbeiʃən/ *n.* 扰动，波动

日子到了 5 月中旬，依照我那简陋的木头日历来计算，大概是 5 月 16 日（我到现在为止还是把一切都记在那根木柱子上）那天，刮了一整天的大风，又是打闪，又是打雷，来势凶猛，夜里还风雨交加，一直不停。我也说不清那会儿是什么时刻，只记得我正在阅读《圣经》，还认真地考虑自己眼下的处境，忽然传来一声枪响，好像是从海上传来的，这使我大吃一惊。我以超乎想像的速度很快跳了出来，并且立刻把梯子竖在山坡上，登上山坡后，又把梯子收起来，第二次爬上梯子，登上了那座小山的山顶。就在刹那间，我看见火光一闪，说明响了第二枪，果然半分钟以后，我听见了枪声。从声音可以推断出，这是从上回我坐船被急流冲走的那一带海上传来的。

⑤ foul /faul/ *a.*（天气）恶劣的

⑥ trice /trais/ *n.* 瞬间，顷刻

⑦ clap /klæp/ *v.* 急速处理，用力地放

time, got to the top of the hill the very moment that a **flash**[①] of fire **bid**[②] me listen for a second gun, which, accordingly, in about half a minute I heard; and by the sound, knew that it was from that part of the sea where I was driven down the current in my boat.

And when it was broad day, and the air cleared up, I saw something at a great distance at sea, full east of the island, whether a sail or a **hull**[③] I could not distinguish—no, not with my glass: the distance was so great, and the weather still something **hazy**[④] also; at least, it was so out at sea.

And being eager, you may be sure, to be satisfied, I took my gun in my hand, and ran towards the south side of the island to the rocks where I had formerly been carried away by the current; and getting up there, the weather by this time being perfectly clear, I could plainly see, to my great sorrow, the **wreck**[⑤] of a ship, cast away in the night upon those **concealed**[⑥] rocks which I found when I was out in my boat.

I cannot explain, by any possible energy of words, what a strange longing I felt in my soul upon this sight, breaking out sometimes thus: "Oh that there had been but one or two, nay, or but one soul saved out of this ship, to have escaped to me, that I might but have had one companion, one fellow-creature, to have spoken to me and to have **conversed**[⑦] with! " In all the time of my **solitary**[⑧] life I never felt so earnest, so strong a desire after the **society**[⑨] of my fellow-creatures, or so deep a regret at the want of it.

I believe I repeated the words, "Oh that it had been but one! " a thousand times.

It was now calm, and I had a great mind to venture out in my boat to this wreck, not doubting but I might find something on board that

① flash /flæʃ/ *n.* 闪光，闪现
② bid /bid/ *v.* 命令，吩咐

等到天色大亮，海上开始晴朗的时候，在海岛正东方远处海面上，我仿佛看见一个什么东西，究竟是船还是帆，却不太清楚，甚至用望远镜望去都没有办法，因为距离太远，并且海上有雾气——海上一贯如此。

③ hull /hʌl/ *n.* 壳，船体
④ hazy /'heizi/ *a.* 朦胧的，烟雾弥漫的

你也能够相信，我总是急于想把事情搞个水落石出，于是就手里拿着枪向这座岛屿南部跑去，跑到我上回被激流冲走的那些岩石前面。等我跑到了那里时，天色到已经大亮了，最让我感到难过的是，我一眼看出，有一只失事的大船，昨天夜里撞在我以前驾舟出游时发现的那些暗礁上。

⑤ wreck /rek/ *n.* 残骸
⑥ conceal /kən'siːl/ *v.* 隐藏

看到这些景象，我也不知道为什么，此刻我内心中忽然产生一种稀奇古怪的、寻找朋友的强烈要求，有时我禁不住大声疾呼："天哪，哪怕只有一两个人，不，哪怕只有一个人从这艘船上逃命出来也好啊！这样也好让我有一个伴侣，有一个同类的人说说话、交谈交谈啊！"多年来我一直过着孤独的生活，从来没有像今天一样渴望有人往来，也从来没有像今天这样深切地感到没有伴侣的痛苦。

⑦ converse /kən'vəːs/ *v.* 交谈，谈话
⑧ solitary /'sɔlitəri/ *a.* 孤独的
⑨ society /sə'saiəti/ *n.* 交际，社交

"啊，哪怕只有一个人呢！"我一直重复着这句话，至少念叨了一千遍。

海上已经风平浪静，我心里很想冒险乘坐自己的那只小船到那条破船上，确信我可以从那只破船上找到一些对自己有用的东西。同时，还有一种动机在更有力地推动着我，就是希望我还可

might be useful to me. But that did not altogether press me so much as the possibility that there might be yet some living creature on board, whose life I might not only save, but might, by saving that life, comfort my own to the last degree.

But having a strong **steerage**① with my paddle, I went at a great rate directly for the wreck, and in less than two hours I came up to it. When I came close to her, a dog appeared upon her, who, seeing me coming, **yelped**② and cried; and as soon as I called him, jumped into the sea to come to me. I took him into the boat, but found him almost dead with hunger and thirst. I gave him a cake of my bread, and he devoured it like a ravenous wolf that had been starving a **fortnight**③ in the snow; I then gave the poor creature some fresh water, with which, if I would have let him, he would have burst himself. After this I went on board. Besides the dog, there was nothing left in the ship that had life; nor any goods, that I could see, but what were spoiled by the water.

In the wreck I had been so near obtaining what I so earnestly longed for—somebody to speak to, and to learn some knowledge from them of the place where I was, and of the probable means of my deliverance. I was **agitated**④ wholly by these thoughts; all my calm of mind, in my **resignation**⑤ to **Providence**⑥, and waiting the issue of the **dispositions**⑦ of Heaven, seemed to be **suspended**⑧; and I had as it were no power to turn my thoughts to anything but to the project of a voyage to the main, which came upon me with such force, and such an **impetuosity**⑨ of desire, that it was not to be resisted.

My only way to go about to attempt an escape was, if possible, to get a savage into my possession; and, if possible, it should be one of

以拯救出船上活着的一两个人，这对我个人至少也是一种安慰。

我以桨代舵，使劲掌握着方向，驾着独木舟朝那条破船飞速驶去，不到两个小时就划到船边。我靠到近处，忽然看见船上有一条狗冲我“汪汪”直叫。我呼唤了它一声，它就跳到海里，游到我的小船这边来。我把它拉到船上，只见它已经快渴死了。我给了它一块面包，它就大吃大嚼起来，就像在雪地里饿了两个星期的狼。我给它喝了点清水，恐怕如果一劲儿给它喝水的话，它就会喝得胀破肚子。随后，我登上了大船。除了那条狗，船上没有一个活的动物，船上的货物也都给水泡坏了。

在那条破船上，我几乎就要如愿以偿了——也就是说，能找到个说话的人，从他们那里了解一下我所待的究竟是什么地方，有没有脱险的办法，但结果却毫无所获。本来我心里很平静，自己只想着听天由命，一切由老天爷来安排，而现在却再也无法静下心来。我好像无法驾驭自己的思绪，整天幻想着如何渡海到那块大陆上去，而且这种念头一直凶猛而强劲地左右着我，简直叫我无法抵抗。

我现在想要逃走的唯一方法就是，如果条件允许的话，尽可能弄到一个野人为我所有，如果可能的话，最好是一个被他们带来准备杀死吃掉的俘虏。

自从有了这种想法以后，我的头脑里总是在

① steerage /'stiəridʒ/ *n.* 把舵
② yelp /jelp/ *v.* 发出短而尖的叫声，叫喊
③ fortnight /'fɔːtnait/ *n.* 两星期
④ agitated /'ædʒiteitid/ *a.* 激动不安的，焦虑的
⑤ resignation /ˌrezig'neiʃən/ *n.* 认命，屈从
⑥ Providence /'prɔvidəns/ *n.* 天意，上帝
⑦ disposition /dispə'ziʃən/ *n.* 处置
⑧ suspend /səs'pend/ *v.* 推迟，暂停，取消
⑨ impetuosity /imˌpetju'ɔsiti/ *n.* 激烈，性急

their prisoners, whom they had condemned to be eaten, and should bring hither to kill.

About a year and a half after I entertained these notions, and by long musing had, as it were, resolved them all into nothing, for want of an occasion to put them into execution, I was surprised one morning by seeing no less than five canoes all on shore together on my side the island, and the people who belonged to them all landed and out of my sight.

Here I observed, by the help of my perspective glass, that they were no less than thirty in number; that they had a fire kindled, and that they had meat dressed. How they had cooked it I knew not, or what it was; but they were all dancing, in I know not how many barbarous gestures and figures, their own way, round the fire.

While I was thus looking on them, I perceived, by my perspective, two miserable wretches **dragged**① from the boats, where, it seems, they were laid by, and were now brought out for the slaughter.

A poor wretch, seeing himself a little at liberty and unbound, with hopes of life, started away from them, and ran with incredible swiftness along the sands, directly towards me. I was dreadfully frightened, I must acknowledge, when I perceived him run my way; and especially when, as I thought, I saw him pursued by the whole body.

However, I kept my station, and my spirits began to recover when I found that there was not above three men that followed him; and still more was I encouraged, when I found that he **outstripped**② them exceedingly in running, and gained ground on them; so that, if he could but hold out for half-an-hour, I saw easily he would fairly get away from them all.

琢磨这件事，可是因为我自己没有机会将其付诸实施，始终没有什么结果。这样大约过了一年半，有一天一大早，我忽然发现有不下5艘独木船一齐向我这座岛屿靠了岸，而且船上所有人都已经登陆了，不知去向。

我借助随身携带的望远镜望去，看出他们的人数不下30个，已经生起火来，他们正在那里烤肉。至于他们如何烤肉以及烤什么，我并不知道。只见他们正在那里用各种各样的我所看不懂的愚昧姿势和步伐，以他们自己的方式围着火堆跳舞。

我正这样看着的时候，我从望远镜中看见他们从小船上拖出两个倒霉的野人来，这两个野人大概是他们预先放在船上，而现在要拿出来屠杀了。

① drag /dræg/ *v.* 拖累，拖拉

一个可怜虫见自己被松了绑，没人注意，起了逃生之念，突然逃出了他们的包围，以惊人的速度沿着海岸往我这边跑。我一见他向我跑来，特别是猛然间一看，所有的野人都在后面追赶，说实话，我可真吓坏了。

不过，我待在原地没动，而当我发现追赶他的不过3个人，我的胆子慢慢大起来。更能振奋勇气的是，我看见那个可怜的受难者比那3个人跑得快得多，而且把他们远远地甩在了后面，只要他再坚持半个小时，就完全有把握逃脱他们的追赶。

② outstrip /aut'strip/ *v.* 超过，跑过

在他们和我的城堡之间，有一条我在前面常提起过的小河。很显然，在我看来那个可怜的野

There was between them and my castle the creek, which I mentioned often in the first part of my story; and this I saw plainly he must necessarily swim over, or the poor wretch would be taken there; but when the savage escaping came thither, he made nothing of it, though the tide was then up, but **plunging**① in, swam through in about thirty strokes, or thereabouts, landed, and ran with exceeding strength and swiftness. When the three persons came to the creek, I found that two of them could swim, but the third could not, and that, standing on the other side, he looked at the others, but went no farther, and soon after went softly back again, which, as it happened, was very well for him in the end.

It came now very warmly upon my thoughts, and indeed **irresistibly**②, that now was the time to get me a servant, and, perhaps, a companion or assistant; and that I was plainly called by Providence to save this poor creature's life. I immediately ran down the ladders with all possible **expedition**③, **fetched**④ my two guns, for they were both at the foot of the ladders, as I observed before, and getting up again with the same haste to the top of the hill, I crossed towards the sea; and having a very short cut, and all down hill, placed myself in the way between the pursuers and the pursued, **hallooing**⑤ aloud to him that fled, who, looking back, was at first perhaps as much frightened at me as at them; but I **beckoned**⑥ with my hand to him to come back; and, in the meantime, I slowly advanced towards the two that followed; then rushing at once upon the foremost, I knocked him down with the stock of my piece.

Having knocked this fellow down, the other who pursued him stopped, as if he had been frightened, and I advanced towards him;

人必须趟过这条河，否则就一定会被他们在河边捉住。尽管河水已经涨了，但那个逃生的野人并不把它当回事，猛地跳了下去，只划了30来下，便游到了对面，爬上岸，快速向前奔跑。当那3个人到了小河边的时候，我发现，他们只有两个人会游水，第三个人可能不会，只好站在河边，看着那两个人过河。没过多久，那个人就悄悄回去了——对他而言，实在是件好事。

此刻，我脑海里忽然闪现出一个强烈的不可抗拒的念头：我要找一个仆人，现在正是时候，很可能我还会找到一个伴侣或帮手呢。这一定是上天召唤我去救这个可怜虫。我立刻以最快的速度下了梯子，拿起我的两枝枪，我在前面说过，这两枝枪就放在梯子脚下，又以同样快的速度爬上梯子，翻过那座小山的山顶，向海边跑去。我抄了一条小路，全力跑下山去，置身于追者和被追者中间。我朝那个逃生的野人大声呼唤。他回头望了望，起初好像怕他们一样很怕我，但是我用手召他回来，同时慢慢地向后面追赶的两个野人迎上去。等我走近他们时，我猛地冲到最前面的那个野人面前，用枪托把他打倒了。

我把第一个野人打倒之后，跟在他后面的那个野人停住了脚步，似乎吓呆了，我便急急赶上去。但是，等我走近他的时候，我一眼就瞧见他手里拿着一副弓箭，正要朝我放箭。因此，我当时不得不先开枪把他打死。那个逃生的野人这时也停住了脚步，亲眼看见了他的两个敌人都已经

① plunge /plʌndʒ/ *v.* 投入，跳进

② irresistibly/ˌiri'zistəbli/ *ad.* 不可抵抗地，压制不住地

③ expedition /ˌekspi'diʃən/ *n.* 迅速

④ fetch /fetʃ/ *v.* 接来，取来

⑤ halloo /hə'lu/*v.* 高呼，喊叫着追赶

⑥ beckon /'bekən/ *v.* 招手

but as I came nearer, I perceived presently he had a bow and arrow, and was fitting it to shoot at me; so I was then obliged to shoot at him first, which I did, and killed him at the first shot. The poor savage who fled, but had stopped, though he saw both his enemies fallen and killed, as he thought, yet was so frightened with the fire and noise of my piece that he stood stock still, and neither came forward nor went backward, though he seemed rather inclined still to fly than to come on. I hallooed again to him, and made signs to come forward, which he easily understood, and came a little way; then stopped again, and then a little farther, and stopped again; and I could then perceive that he stood **trembling**①, as if he had been taken prisoner, and had just been to be killed, as his two enemies were.

At length he came close to me; and then he kneeled down again, kissed the ground, and laid his head upon the ground, and taking me by the foot, set my foot upon his head; this, it seems, was **in token of**② swearing to be my slave for ever.

The savage whom I had knocked down was not killed, but **stunned**③ with the blow, and began to come to himself; so I pointed to him, and showed him the savage, that he was not dead. Upon this my savage, for so I call him now, made a motion to me to lend him my sword, which hung naked in a belt by my side, so I did. He no sooner had it, but he runs to his enemy, and at one blow cut off his head so cleverly, no **executioner**④ in Germany could have done it sooner or better.

He took up his bow and arrows, and came back; so I turned to go away, and beckoned him to follow me, making signs to him that more might come after them. Upon this he made signs to me that he should bury them with sand, that they might not be seen by the rest, if they

倒在地上，想必是死了，又被我的枪声和火光吓坏了，呆呆地站在那里，既不进又不退，但看来还想接着逃，并不想靠过来。我大声招呼他，做手势叫他过来。他已经明白了我的意思，往前走了几步，但是又站住了，然后又走了几步，又站住了。这时候，我能感觉到他站在那里，全身都在发抖，好像成了我的俘虏，要像追赶他的两个敌人一样被杀了。

最后，那个逃生的野人走到我的眼前，然后再跪下去，亲吻着地面，把头贴在地面上，把我的一只脚放在他的头上，看起来好像在发誓要永远做我的奴隶。

我先前打倒的那个野人并没有死，只是给打晕了，现在慢慢清醒过来。于是，我把那个野人指给他看，示意那个追他的野人并没死。这时候，那个逃命的野人向我作了一个动作，请求我把腰间挂得那把没有鞘的刀借给他。于是，我把刀递给了他。他接过我的刀，立刻跑到他的敌人面前，手起刀落，一下子把脑袋砍掉了，即使是德国的刽子手，也不见得比他砍得更快更好。

他把另一个野人的弓箭取了回来，于是我离开那个地方，叫他和我一起走，同时用手势告诉他，后面说不定还会有人追来呢。他懂了我的意思，就向我打手势，表示要把他们用沙土埋起来，免得给后面的野人看见。我打手势叫他照办。他只用了一刻钟，就把那两个野人都埋上了。于是，我便叫他走。

① tremble /ˈtrembl/ *v.* 战慄，忧虑

② in token of 表示，作为……的标志

③ stun /stʌn/ *v.* 使晕倒，使惊吓

④ executioner /ˌeksiˈkjuːʃənə/ *n.* 刽子手

followed; and so I made signs to him again to do so. I believe he had him buried them both in a quarter of an hour. Then, I called him away.

Here I gave him bread and a bunch of raisins to eat, and a **draught**[①] of water, which I found he was indeed in great distress for, from his running.

He was a **comely**[②], handsome fellow, perfectly well made, with straight, strong **limbs**[③], not too large, tall, and well-shaped, and, as I reckon, about twenty-six years of age.

In a little time I began to speak to him; and teach him to speak to me; and first, I let him know his name should be Friday, which was the day I saved his life: I called him so for the memory of the time. I likewise taught him to say Master; and then let him know that was to be my name; I likewise taught him to say Yes and No and to know the meaning of them.

I kept there with him all that night; but as soon as it was day I beckoned to him to come with me, and let him know I would give him some clothes. I then led him up to the top of the hill, to see if his enemies were gone; and pulling out my glass I looked, and saw plainly the place where they had been, but no appearance of them or their canoes.

But I was not content with this discovery; but having now more courage, and consequently more curiosity, I took my man Friday with me, giving him the sword in his hand, with the bow and arrows at his back, which I found he could use very dexterously, making him carry one gun for me, and I two for myself; and away we marched to the place where these creatures had been; for I had a mind now to get some further intelligence of them. When I came to the place my very

到洞里，我给了他一些面包和一串葡萄干吃，又给他点水喝，因为我见他跑了半天，已经饥渴不堪了。

① draught /drɑːft / *n.* 一口

他是一个眉目俊秀、身材适中的小伙子，有着既细长又结实的四肢，但并不粗大。他个子高，长得很匀称，年龄大约 26 岁。

② comely /'kʌmli/ *a.* 清秀的，标致的
③ limb /lim/ *n.* 肢，臂，腿

不久，我尝试着与他说话，并教他与我说话。首先，我让他知道他叫“星期五”，因为我在星期五救了他的命，而我这样叫他，是为了纪念这个日子。我也教会他说“主人”，然后让他知道，这就算是我的名字。我又教他说“是”和“不是”，并且让他知道它们的含意。

当天晚上我和他在地洞里过了夜，天刚亮，我就召唤他跟我走，同时让他知道我要给他一些衣服。然后我又把他带到小山顶上，看看那些野人走了没有。我拿起望远镜望去，首先看见了那帮野人昨天聚集的地方，可是不见了那群野人和他们的独木船。

但是，我对这种发现并不满足。我现在的勇气更多，好奇心更大。我叫我的仆人星期五手里拿着刀，背上背着弓箭（现在，我已经知道星期五是一个箭法很娴熟的弓箭手。），又叫他替我背上一枝枪，我自己背了两枝枪，一起向那群野人曾聚集过的地方出发，因为我想更详细地了解他们，获得更充分的情报。到了那里，我一看到那片惨绝人寰的景象，全身发冷，心脏都要停止跳动。那真是一幅可怕的景象！至

blood ran **chill**[1] in my veins, and my heart sunk within me, at the horror of the spectacle; indeed, it was a dreadful sight, at least it was so to me, though Friday made nothing of it.

I caused Friday to gather all the skulls, bones, flesh, and whatever remained, and lay them together in a heap, and make a great fire upon it, and burn them all to ashes.

When he had done this, we came back to our castle.

But to return to my new companion. I was greatly delighted with him, and made it my business to teach him everything that was proper to make him useful, handy, and helpful; but especially to make him speak, and understand me when I spoke.

This was the pleasantest year of all the life I led in this place. Friday began to talk pretty well, and understand the names of almost everything I had occasion to call for, and of every place I had to send him to, and talked a great deal to me.

After Friday and I became more **intimately**[2] acquainted, and that he could understand almost all I said to him, and speak pretty fluently, though in broken English, to me, I acquainted him with my own history, or at least so much of it as related to my coming to this place: how I had lived there, and how long; I let him into the mystery, for such it was to him, of gunpowder and bullet, and taught him how to shoot.

I described to him the country of Europe, particularly England, which I came from; how we lived, how we **worshipped**[3] God, how we behaved to one another, and how we traded in ships to all parts of the world. I gave him an account of the wreck which I had been on board of, and showed him, as near as I could, the place where she lay; but

① chill /tʃil/ *a.* 寒冷的，冷漠的

少在我看来是这么一种感觉，但在星期五眼里，那算不了什么。

我让星期五把所有的骷髅、人骨、人肉以及其他剩下的东西收集成一堆，点火把它们烧成灰烬。

我们把事情办完后回到了城堡。

现在回过头来，让我谈谈我的新伙伴星期五。我对他十分满意，我认为我应该把各种事情都教给他，让他成为我的得力助手，特别是要教会他说话，当我说话时，让他明白我的意思。

这是我来到岛上以后过得最愉快的一年。星期五渐渐地会说话了，差不多能完全明白我所要他拿的每一样东西的名字，懂得我差他去的每一个地方，而且一天到晚跟我谈话。

② intimately /ˈintimitli/ *ad.* 密切地，熟悉地

我和星期五更加熟识以后，等到他差不多能够完全听懂我所说的话，并且能够用断断续续的英语流利地与我交谈之后，我就把我的经历告诉了他，特别是我怎样来到岛上，怎样在岛上生活，以及生活了多久等等。我又把子弹和火药的秘密——他认为的秘密，告诉了他，并且教会他如何开枪。

③ worship /ˈwəːʃip/ *v.* 崇拜，敬仰

我把欧洲的情形，特别是我的故乡英国的情形告诉了他，并且向他讲述了我们怎样生活，怎样崇拜上帝，怎样彼此相处，怎样乘船到世界各地去做生意。我把我所乘的船出事的经过告诉了他，尽可能指出那条破船从前在的地方。那条船早已被风浪打得粉碎，连影子都没有了。我又把我们逃命时翻掉的那只小艇的残骸指给他看。我曾

she was all beaten in pieces before, and gone. I showed him the ruins of our boat, which we lost when we escaped, and which I could not stir with my whole strength then; but was now fallen almost all to pieces. Upon seeing this boat, Friday stood, musing a great while, and said nothing. I asked him what it was he studied upon. At last says he, "Me see such boat like come to place at my nation."

Friday described the boat to me well enough; but brought me better to understand him when he added with some warmth, "We save the white mans from drown." Then I presently asked if there were any white mans, as he called them, in the boat. "Yes," he said; "the boat full of white mans." I asked him how many. He told upon his fingers seventeen. I asked him then what became of them. He told me, "They live, they **dwell**① at my nation."

This put new thoughts into my head; for I presently imagined that these might be the men belonging to the ship that was cast away in the sight of my island, as I now called it; and who, after the ship was struck on the rock, and they saw her **inevitably**② lost, had saved themselves in their boat, and were landed upon that wild shore among the savages. Upon this I inquired of him more critically what was become of them. He assured me they lived still there; that they had been there about four years; that the savages left them alone, and gave them **victuals**③ to live on. I asked him how it came to pass they did not kill them and eat them. He said, "No, they make brother with them; "

I was busy one morning upon something of this kind, when I called to Friday, and bid him to go to the sea-shore and see if he could find a turtle or a tortoise, a thing which we generally got once a week, for the sake of the eggs as well as the flesh. Friday had not been long gone

经使出全部气力去移动它，它却丝毫未动，现在也快烂成碎片了。星期五一看到那只小艇，一句话也不说，站在那里出神。我问星期五在想什么，最后他说："我见过这样的小艇到我们国里来。"

星期五把那只小艇的情况向我讲得很详细，这使我更好地明白了他的意思，接着他又补充了一些让人心慰的话。后来他又补充说："我们又从水里救出来一些白人。"我立刻问星期五那艘艇上是否有白人。他说："有满满一船白人。"我问他有多少，他用他的手指头告诉我，一共有 17 个人。我又问到他们的下落，他告诉我："他们住在我们国里。"

他的这番话使我产生了新的想法。我马上联想到，这批人可能就是我从岛上亲眼看见它出事的那条大船上的船员。他们在大船触礁之后，知道大船一定要沉没，都逃到小艇上去了，在那片有野人的陆地登岸。因此，我又仔细向星期五打听那群白人的下落。他再三告诉我，那些白人现在还住在那里，已经在那里居住了 4 年了。野人们并不去打扰，而且还供给他们粮食。我问星期五，他们为什么不把那些白人杀死吃掉呢？他说："我们大家成了兄弟。"

有一天早晨，我自己正忙于干别的事情，不能脱身，于是就让星期五到海边去，看看能不能找到一只海龟，因为我们每星期总要出去一次弄一个回来，为的是吃它的蛋和肉。星期五去后不多一会儿，很快就飞跑回来。星期五一纵身就跳

① dwell /dwel/ *v.* 居住

② inevitably /in'evitəbli/ *ad.* 不可避免地

③ victual /'vitl/ *n.* 食物

when he came running back, and flew over my outer wall or fence, like one that felt not the ground or the steps he set his foot on; and before I had time to speak to him he cries out to me, "O master! O master! O sorrow! O bad!"—"What's the matter, Friday?" says I. "O **yonder**[①] there," says he, "one, two, three canoes; one, two, three!" By this way of speaking I concluded there were six; but on inquiry I found there were but three. "Well, Friday," says I, "do not be frightened." So I heartened him up as well as I could.

So I went and fetched a good dram of rum and gave him. When he had drunk it, I made him take the two fowling-pieces, which we always carried, and loaded them with large **swan-shot**[②], as big as small pistol-bullets. Then I took four muskets, and loaded them with two **slugs**[③] and five small bullets each; and my two pistols I loaded with a brace of bullets each. I hung my great sword, as usual, naked by my side, and gave Friday his hatchet. When I had thus prepared myself, I took my perspective glass, and went up to the side of the hill, to see what I could discover; and I found quickly by my glass that there were twenty-one savages, three prisoners, and three canoes; and that their whole business seemed to be the **triumphant**[④] banquet upon these three human bodies: a barbarous feast, indeed! but nothing more than, as I had observed, was usual with them.

In this **fit**[⑤] of fury I divided the arms which I had charged, as before, between us; I gave Friday one pistol to stick in his girdle, and three guns upon his shoulder, and I took one pistol and the other three guns myself; and in this posture we marched out.

With this resolution I entered the wood, and, with all possible **wariness**[⑥] and silence, Friday following close at my heels, I marched

进了外墙，似乎脚不曾着地。我还没有开口说话，星期五就冲我喊道："主人，主人，坏了！坏了！"我说："出了什么事，星期五？"星期五说："那边有一条、两条、三条独木船。一条，两条，三条！"我刚听了星期五这么说，还以为有6条船呢；再问才知道只有3条独木船。我说："不要害怕，星期五。"我尽量帮助他壮壮胆子。

于是，我拿了一杯甘蔗酒给他喝。等他把酒喝下去，我叫他去取我们平常携带的两枝鸟枪，把它们装上大号的子弹——就像手枪子弹那么大。接着我自己也取了4枝短枪，每枝短枪里装了两颗斜形弹和5颗小子弹，又把我的两把手枪装上了子弹。此外，我把大刀挂在腰上，与往常一样，不带刀鞘，同时把斧子交给星期五。等这些准备妥当以后，我就拿了望远镜，跑到山坡上去观察那些野人在干什么。从望远镜中，我一眼就看出，一共有21个野人，3个俘虏，3艘独木船，而且看样子，这些野人的任务大概是要拿这3个活人开一次胜利宴会。这是一种非常野蛮残忍的人肉大餐，但对于这些野人，正如我所观察的，他们都习以为常了。

在这种怒火中烧的心情下，我把我早已装好的武器分成两份，交给星期五一把手枪，让他插在腰带上，又叫他背上3杆长枪。我自己也拿了一把手枪和3杆长枪。我们武装好了之后就出发了。

这样决定以后，我就进入了树林里，告诉星期五紧跟在我的背后，极其小心谨慎地、静悄悄

① yonder /'jɔndə/ *a.* 那边的，远处的

② swan-shot *n.* 猎射天鹅用的大子弹

③ slug /slʌg/ *n.* 子弹，金属小块

④ triumphant /trai'ʌmfənt/ *a.* 得胜的，得意扬扬的

⑤ fit /fit/ *n.* 发作，一阵

⑥ wariness /'weərinis/ *n.* 注意，小心

till I came to the **skirts**① of the wood on the side which was next to them, only that one corner of the wood lay between me and them. Here I called softly to Friday, and showing him a great tree which was just at the corner of the wood, I bade him go to the tree, and bring me word if he could see there plainly what they were doing. He did so, and came immediately back to me, and told me they might be plainly viewed there—that they were all about their fire, eating the flesh of one of their prisoners, and that another lay bound upon the sand a little from them, whom he said they would kill next; and this fired the very soul within me. He told me it was not one of their nation, but one of the bearded men he had told me of, that came to their country in the boat. I was filled with horror at the very naming of the white bearded man; and going to the tree, I saw plainly by my glass a white man, who lay upon the beach of the sea with his hands and his feet tied with flags, or things like **rushes**②, and that he was an European, and had clothes on.

I had now not a moment to lose, for nineteen of the dreadful wretches sat upon the ground, all close huddled together, and had just sent the other two to **butcher**③ the poor Christian, and bring him perhaps limb by limb to their fire, and they were stooping down to untie the bands at his feet. I turned to Friday. "Now, Friday," said I, "do as I bid thee."; then asking him if he was ready, he said, "Yes." "Then fire at them," said I; and at the same moment I fired also.

Friday took his aim so much better than I, that on the side that he shot he killed two of them, and wounded three more; and on my side I killed one, and wounded two. They were, you may be sure, in a dreadful **consternation**④: and all of them that were not hurt jumped

① skirts /skəːts/ *n.* 边缘，边界

② rush /rʌʃ/ *n.* 灯芯草

③ butcher /ˈbutʃə/ *v.* 屠宰，屠杀

④ consternation /ˌkɔnstə(ː)ˈneiʃən/ *n.* 惊愕，惊惶失措

地往前走，一直走到树林的边缘。那个地方离那些野人最近，中间只隔着枝林的一个角。一到了那里，我就悄悄地招呼星期五，指着树林边最靠外的一棵大树，吩咐他到树后去看看，如果能看清楚他们的活动情况，就回来告诉我。他去了不久就回来告诉我说，那个地方看得很清楚，那帮野人正围坐在火堆边，吃着一个俘虏的肉；还有一个俘虏躺在离那群野人不远的沙滩上，手脚被捆绑着，据星期五猜测，那个俘虏很快要就被杀了。听了这话之后，我不禁怒火万丈。星期五告诉我，那个俘虏并非他们同族，而是他曾经与我说过的、坐小船来到他们国家的那种有胡子的人。我听说是有胡子的白人，不禁大吃一惊。我走到那棵树之后，用望远镜一望，果然清清楚楚地看见一个白人躺在沙滩上，手脚被灯芯草之类的东西捆绑着，同时可以看出他是个欧洲人，身上穿着衣服。

现在已经到了紧急时刻，因为我看见 19 个野人围坐在一起，他们已经派出两个野人去屠宰那个可怜的白人俘虏，大概要把他肢解成几块。我看到那两个野人已经弯下腰，正在解那个白人俘虏脚上绑的东西。我对星期五说："你照我的样子做。"我问他是否准备好了，他说："好了。"我说："向他们开火吧。"我同时也开了枪。

星期五枪法要比我好得多，他那边打死了两个，打伤了 3 个，而我这边只打死了一个，伤了两个。不用说，你也会相信，那群野人顿时被吓得魂飞天外，那些没有被打死打伤的都一齐跳了

upon their feet, but did not immediately know which way to run, or which way to look, for they knew not from whence their destruction came.

"Now, Friday," says I, laying down the **discharged**① pieces, and taking up the musket which was yet loaded, "follow me," which he did with a great deal of courage; upon which I rushed out of the wood and showed myself, and Friday close at my foot. As soon as I perceived they saw me, I shouted as loud as I could, and bade Friday do so too, and running as fast as I could, which, by the way, was not very fast, being loaded with arms as I was, I made directly towards the poor **victim**②.

The two butchers who were just going to work with him had left him at the surprise of our first fire, and fled in a terrible fright to the seaside, and had jumped into a canoe, and three more of the rest made the same way. I turned to Friday, and bade him step forwards and fire at them.

While my man Friday fired at them, I pulled out my knife and cut the flags that bound the poor victim; and loosing his hands and feet, I lifted him up, and asked him in the Portuguese tongue what he was. He answered in Latin, Christianus. "Seignior," said I, with as much Spanish as I could make up, "we will talk afterwards, but we must fight now: if you have any strength left, take this pistol and sword, and lay about you." He took them very thankfully; and no sooner had he the arms in his hands, but, as if they had put new vigour into him, he flew upon his murderers like a fury, and had cut two of them in pieces.

Friday, being now left to his liberty, pursued the flying wretches, with no weapon in his hand but his hatchet: and with that he

起来，也不知道往哪里跑，不知道往哪里看，因为他们根本不知道这场灾难从何处降临。

我把放过了的枪放下，把那把装好了子弹的手枪拿在手里，对星期五说："星期五，你跟我来。"他果然很勇敢地跟着我。我冲出树林，出现在了那群野人前面。星期五与我紧紧相随。当他们发现我时，我就拼命喊叫，也叫星期五大声呐喊。我一边大声喊叫，一边向那个可怜的白人俘虏跑去，但因为身上所背的枪械太重，跑得并不算快。

① discharged /dis'tʃaːdʒd/ *a.* 子弹打完的

那两个正要动手宰杀那个白人俘虏的野人，在我们放头一枪的时候，就已被吓得魂不附体，丢开了那个白人俘虏向海边跑去，跳上了一只独木船，此外还有 3 个野人也朝同一方向跑去。我转身告诉星期五，叫他追过去向他们开枪。

② victim /'viktim/ *n.* 受害者

在星期五向那几个野人开火的时候，我拔出刀子，把那位可怜的白人俘虏身上捆着的灯芯草割断，给他手脚松了绑，然后把他扶起来，用葡萄牙语问他是什么人。他用拉丁语回答说："基督徒。""先生，"我把我所知道的西班牙话通通搬了出来，"我们过会儿再谈吧，现在打仗要紧。要是你还有点力气的话，你就拿着这把手枪和这把刀杀过去吧。"他非常感激地接了过去。他一拿到武器，仿佛增加了无穷的力量，立刻向那些野人冲了过去，一下子砍倒了两个，把他们剁成了肉泥。

星期五趁此时没人管他，立刻把武器丢在一边，只拿了一把斧子，向那些望风而逃的野人追去。星期五用斧子砍死了 3 个受伤的野人，并且

despatched[①] those three who as I said before, were wounded at first and fallen, and all the rest he could come up with; and the **Spaniard**[②] coming to me for a gun, I gave him one of the fowling-pieces, with which he pursued two of the savages, and wounded them both; but as he was not able to run, they both got from him into the wood, where Friday pursued them, and killed one of them, but the other was too nimble for him; and though he was wounded, yet had plunged himself into the sea, and swam with all his **might**[③] off to those two who were left in the canoe; which three in the canoe, with one wounded, that we knew not whether he died or no, were all that escaped our hands of twenty-one.

Those that were in the canoe worked hard to get out of gun-shot. So I consented to pursue them by sea, and running to one of their canoes, I jumped in and bade Friday follow me, but when I was in the canoe I was surprised to find another poor creature lie there alive, bound hand and foot, as the Spaniard was, for the slaughter.

I immediately cut the **twisted**[④] flags or rushes which they had bound him with, and would have helped him up; but he could not stand or speak, but **groaned**[⑤] most **piteously**[⑥], believing, it seems, still, that he was only unbound in order to be killed. When Friday came to him I bade him speak to him, and tell him of his deliverance; and pulling out my bottle, made him give the poor wretch a dram, which, with the news of his being delivered, revived him, and he sat up in the boat. But when Friday came to hear him speak, and look in his face, it would have moved any one to tears to have seen how Friday kissed him, embraced him, hugged him, like a **distracted**[⑦] creature. It was a good while before I could make him speak to me or tell me what was

① despatch /dis'pætʃ/ *v.* (迅速) 处决，杀死

② Spaniard /'spænjəd/ *n.* 西班牙人

把能够追得上的野人一律斩尽杀绝。这时候，那个西班牙人跑来向我要枪，我就给了他一枝鸟枪。那个西班牙人拿着鸟枪追上了两个野人，把他们打伤了。但由于那个西班牙人跑不动，那两个野人逃进了树林里。星期五追进了树林里，砍死了一个野人，而另一个野人行动异常敏捷，虽然受了伤，依旧跳入海内，使出平生之力，朝那两个留在木船上的野人游去。在来岛屿的 21 个野人当中，只有这 3 个人，连同一个负伤而又生死不明的野人，从我们的手中逃了出去。

③ might /mait/ *n.* 力量，威力

那几个在独木船上的，拼命想划出我们的射程之外。我立刻跳上一只独木船，吩咐星期五跟我一起上去。但当我跳上这只独木船的时候，却出人意料地发现，船上还躺着另外一个没有死的俘虏，也像那个西班牙人一样，手脚被捆绑着，等待着被宰杀。

④ twisted /'twistid/ *a.* 扭曲的

⑤ groan /grəun/ *v.* 呻吟

⑥ piteously /'pitiəsli/ *ad.* 可怜地，凄惨地

我立刻把捆在他身上的灯芯草等东西割断。我想把他扶起来，但他不能站起来，甚至连说话的力气都没有，只会一个劲儿地哼哼。看起来，他以为我们为他松了绑他就要被屠宰呢。等星期五过来之后，我让星期五告诉这个受难者，他已经获救了。同时我又掏出酒瓶来，叫星期五给他喝几口。他听见自己已经遇救的消息，不觉精神一振，居然在船上坐了起来。不料，星期五一听见那个野人说话就赶紧过来了，一看他的脸，立刻又是吻他，又是拥抱他，像个疯子。那种场景，任何人看了都会被感动得掉泪。足足有半天，我才使得星期五开口，并且告诉了我事情的缘由，

⑦ distracted /dis'træktid/ *a.* 心烦意乱的

the matter; but when he came a little to himself he told me that it was his father.

This affair put an end to our pursuit of the canoe with the other savages, who were now almost out of sight.

My island was now **peopled**①, and I thought myself very rich in subjects; and it was a merry reflection, which I frequently made, how like a king I looked. First of all, the whole country was my own property, so that I had an undoubted right of **dominion**②. Secondly, my people were perfectly **subjected** ③—I was absolutely lord and lawgiver—they all owed their lives to me, and were ready to lay down their lives, if there had been occasion for it, for me. It was remarkable, too, I had but three subjects, and they were of three different religions—my man Friday was a **Protestant**④, his father was a **Pagan**⑤ and a **cannibal**⑥, and the Spaniard was a **Papist**⑦. However, I allowed liberty of conscience throughout my dominions. But this is by the way.

Having now society enough, and our numbers being sufficient to put us out of fear of the savages, if they had come, unless their number had been very great, we went freely all over the island, whenever we found occasion; and as we had our escape or deliverance upon our thoughts, it was impossible, at least for me, to have the means of it out of mine. For this purpose I marked out several trees, which I thought fit for our work, and I set Friday and his father to cut them down; and then I caused the Spaniard, to whom I **imparted**⑧ my thoughts on that affair, to oversee and direct their work.

At the same time I contrived to increase my little flock of tame goats as much as I could.

当他慢慢镇静过来，他告诉我，这是他的父亲。

这件事情的发生，使我们停止了对那条独木船上的野人的追击。他们已跑得无影无踪。

我这座岛屿已经有了居民，我感到我已非常富有，有了不少臣民。我兴奋地想像我多么像一位国王。第一，全岛都是我个人的财产，因此我具有一种毫无疑义的领土权；第二，我的百姓完全服从我，我是他们的全权统治者和立法者。他们都是我救出来的，如果有必要，他们一定会为了我一人而奉献出自己的生命。此外有一件不同寻常的事，那就是我只有 3 个臣民，他们却分属于 3 种不同的宗教：星期五是个新教徒，他的父亲是一个吃人部族的异教徒，而西班牙人又是一个天主教徒。不过，在我的领土上，我允许信仰自由，这是次要的事。

我们现在已经有了足够的人手，即使那群野人过来，我们也不会害怕，除非他们来的人特别多。因此，我们在岛上的各处自由往来，而且因为我们满脑子都在考虑逃走和脱险的事情，说“我们都在考虑”虽不大可能，但我本人确是一直在想着这件事。我们无时无刻不在想办法。为了达到这个目的，我把几棵适于造船的树作了记号，让星期五和他父亲把它们砍倒，然后把我的想法告诉西班牙人，让西班牙人监督、指挥他们工作。

同时，我千方百计把我的小羊群繁殖起来，增加数量。

现在已是收获季节，我们获得了丰收。我们

① people /'pi:pl/ v. 使住(满)人

② dominion /də'minjən/ n. 领土，主权

③ subject /'sʌbdʒikt/ v. 使屈从于……，使隶属

④ protestant /'prɔtistənt/ n. 新教，新教徒

⑤ pagan /'peigən/ n. 异教徒，无宗教信仰者

⑥ cannibal /'kænibəl/ n. 食人者，吃同类的动物

⑦ papist /'peipist/ n. 教宗制信奉者，天主教徒

⑧ impart /im'pa:t/ v. 传授，告知

It was now harvest, and our crop in good order; for from twenty-two **bushels**[①] of barley we brought in and thrashed out above two hundred and twenty bushels; and the like in proportion of the rice. When we had thus housed and secured our magazine of corn, we fell to work to make more wicker-ware, viz. great baskets, in which we kept it.

And now, having a full supply of food for all the guests I expected, I gave the Spaniard leave to go over to the main, to see what he could do with those he had left behind him there. Under these instructions, the Spaniard and the old savage, the father of Friday, went away in one of the canoes which they might be said to have come in, or rather were brought in, when they came as prisoners to be devoured by the savages.

It was no less than eight days I had waited for them, when a strange and unforeseen accident **intervened**[②], of which the like has not, perhaps, been heard of in history.

I was fast asleep in my **hutch**[③] one morning, when my man Friday came running in to me, and called aloud, "Master, master, they are come, they are come!" I jumped up, and regardless of danger, I went, as soon as I could get my clothes on, through my little grove, which, by the way, was by this time grown to be a very thick wood; I say, regardless of danger I went without my arms, which was not my **custom**[④] to do; but I was surprised when, turning my eyes to the sea, I presently saw a boat at about a league and a half distance, standing in for the shore, with a shoulder-of-mutton sail, as they call it, and the wind blowing pretty fair to bring them in; also I observed, presently, that they did not come from that side which the shore lay on, but from

种下22蒲式耳大麦，居然收割并打出来220多蒲式耳，稻子的收成也与此差不多。我们把谷物收藏好之后，大家开始着手那就是编一些大柳条筐子来装它们。

① bushel /'buʃl/ n. 蒲式耳（容量等于8加仑或36.4公升）

现在既然有充分的粮食来款待我期待的客人，我决定让那个西班牙人到大陆上去一趟，看看能不能想个办法帮助那批滞留在那儿的西班牙人过来。那个西班牙人和那个老野人即星期五的父亲接受了我的指示，乘坐一只独木船走了。当初那伙野人把他们当作俘虏载到岛上来，准备把他们吃掉的时候，就是用的这条独木船。

他们走了以后，我刚刚等到第八天的时候，忽然发生了一件意外的事情，这件事不仅奇特怪异，而且也许是有史已来闻所未闻。

② intervene /ˌintə'viːn/ v. 调停，干涉

③ hutch /hʌtʃ/ n. 棚屋

一天清早，我在茅舍里睡得正香，星期五向我跑来，而且大喊："主人，主人，他们来了，他们来了！"我迅速爬了起来，连忙披上衣服，不顾危险跑了出去，穿过小树林，如今它已长成了一片密林；我说的不顾危险意思是我没带任何武器，而这不符合我的日常习惯。当我放眼向海上眺望时，不由得大吃一惊，我看见大约一海里半之外，有一条挂着被称之为"羊肩帆"的小船正在向岸边驶来，劲吹的风恰好把它们送到这边。接着我还注意到，它并不是从大陆那边过来的，而是从岛的南端来的。因此，我把星期五叫进来，并且告诫他不要离开我，因为这些人并不是我们所期待的人，我们还不知道他们是敌人还

④ custom /'kʌstəm/ n. 习惯，风俗

the southernmost end of the island. Upon this I called Friday in, and bade him lie close, for these were not the people we looked for, and that we might not know yet whether they were friends or enemies. In the next place I went in to fetch my perspective glass to see what I could make of them.

I had scarce set my foot upon the hill when my eye plainly discovered a ship lying at anchor, at about two leagues and a half distance from me, south-south-east, but not above a league and a half from the shore. By my observation it appeared plainly to be an English ship, and the boat appeared to be an English long-boat.

I had not kept myself long in this posture till I saw the boat draw near the shore, as if they looked for a creek to **thrust**[①] in at, for the convenience of landing.

When they were on shore I was fully satisfied they were Englishmen; there were in all eleven men, whereof three of them I found were unarmed and, as I thought, bound; and when the first four or five of them were jumped on shore, they took those three out of the boat as prisoners; one of the three I could perceive using the most passionate gestures of entreaty, affliction, and despair, even to a kind of **extravagance**[②]; the other two, I could perceive, lifted up their hands sometimes, and appeared concerned indeed, but not to such a degree as the first.

All this while I had no thought of what the matter really was, but stood trembling with the horror of the sight, expecting every moment when the three prisoners should be killed.

After I had observed the outrageous usage of the three men by the **insolent**[③] seamen, I observed the fellows run **scattering**[④] about the

是朋友。随后我进去把望远镜拿了出来，想弄清楚他们究竟是些什么人。

我刚刚爬上小山，一下子就看见在我前方的东南偏南的方向停留着一条大船，离我大约有七八英里的距离，但是离海岸最多只有四五英里的样子。据我判断，那分明是一条英国船，而那只小船看样子也是一只英国长艇。

我在小山上望了没多久，就见那只小船开到海岸边，似乎正在寻找能把船开进来、便于上岸的港湾。

他们上岸以后，我确信他们都是英国人。他们一共有 11 个人，其中 3 个看样子没有带武器，并且在我看来似乎是被绑着的。船刚靠岸，就有四五个人先跳上了岸来，把囚犯模样的这 3 个人押下了船。我看见 3 人中有一个人正在指手划脚、甚至有些过于夸张地做出种种恳求、悲痛和失望等动作。同时，我看见另外两个人，有时也举起双手，作出很痛苦的样子，但没有第一个人那么激动。

我始终想不出这究竟是怎么回事，只是站在那里，由于刚才所见到的可怕一幕而瑟瑟发抖，每时每刻担心着那 3 个人被杀掉。

我看见那伙气势汹汹的水手把那 3 个人粗暴虐待了一番之后，都在岛上散开了，他们似乎想要察看这个地方的情况。

就在这些人上岸的时候，正是潮水涨得最高的时候。他们中一部分人站着与那 3 个他们带来

① thrust /θrʌst/ *v.* 插入，推挤

② extravagance /ik'strævəgəns/ *n.* 夸张

③ insolent /'insələnt/ *a.* 粗野的，无礼的

④ scatter /'skætə/ *v.* 散开

island, as if they wanted to see the country.

It was just at high-water when these people came on shore; and while partly they stood talking with the prisoners, partly they rambled about to see what kind of a place they were in; they had carelessly stayed till the tide was spent, and the water was ebbed considerably away, leaving their boat aground.

It was my design, as I said above, not to have made any attempt till it was dark; but about two o'clock, being the heat of the day, I found that they were all gone straggling into the woods, and, as I thought, laid down to sleep. The three poor distressed men, too anxious for their condition to get any sleep, had, however, sat down under the shelter of a great tree, at about a quarter of a mile from me, and, as I thought, out of sight of any of the rest. Upon this I resolved to discover myself to them, and learn something of their condition; immediately I marched as above, my man Friday at a good distance behind me, as **formidable**① for his arms as I, but not making quite so **staring**② a **spectre**③-like figure as I did.

"Gentlemen," said I, "do not be surprised at me; perhaps you may have a friend near when you did not expect it." "He must be sent directly from heaven then," said one of them very gravely to me, and pulling off his hat at the same time to me, "for our condition is past the help of man." "All help is from heaven, sir," said I, "but can you put a stranger in the way to help you? for you seem to be in some great distress. I saw you when you landed; and when you seemed to **make application to**④ the **brutes**⑤ that came with you, I saw one of them lift up his sword to kill you."

The poor man, with tears running down his face, and trembling,

的人谈着什么，而另一部分人竟在岛上到处闲逛，看看他们处在一个什么地方。一时大意，居然错过了潮汛，结果海水退得老远，把他们的小船搁浅在沙滩上了。

就如我上面所说，我的计划是在黄昏到来之前不采取任何行动。可是到了下午两点钟左右——天气正热的时候，我看到他们三三两两都跑到树林里，大概是躺下来睡着了。可是那3个可怜的受难者，也许是为自己的处境而焦虑根本睡不着，在一棵大树的浓荫下呆呆地坐着。他们离我大约有四分之一英里远，我想是在其余人的视线之外。看到这种情形，我决定要暴露一下自己，了解一下他们的情况。我向他们走了过去，我的仆人星期五全副武装地跟在后面，与我一样森严可怕。但他那副模样还不至于像我那样简直如同一个两眼发直的怪物。

“各位先生，不要怕我，”我说，“你们面前的也许正是你们不期而至的朋友。”“他一定是上天派下来的，”内中一个人向我脱帽致敬，很认真地对我说，“我们现在的处境恐怕无法挽回了。”“先生，一切挽救来自上天，”我说，“依我所见，你们正处于危险之中，但你们愿意在如此险境接受一个陌生人的帮助吗？你们一上岸我就看见了。当你们向那些一起来的粗暴的家伙哀求的时候，我看见其中有人要举刀杀你们。”

那个可怜的人泪流满面，全身发抖，仿佛十

① formidable /ˈfɔːmidəbl/ *a.* 强大的，可怕的
② staring /ˈstɛəriŋ/ *a.* 显眼的
③ spectre /ˈspektə/ *n.* 鬼怪，恐怖的根源

④ make application to 请求，哀求
⑤ brute /bruːt/ *n.* 畜生，残忍之人

looking like one **astonished**①.

"Our case, sir," said he, "is too long to tell you while our murderers are so near us; but, in short, sir, I was commander of that ship—my men have **mutinied**② against me; they have been hardly prevailed on not to murder me, and, at last, have set me on shore in this **desolate**③ place, with these two men with me—one my mate, the other a passenger—where we expected to perish, believing the place to be uninhabited, and know not yet what to think of it."

"Look you, sir," said I, "if I venture upon your deliverance, are you willing to make two conditions with me?" He **anticipated**④ my proposals by telling me that both he and the ship, if recovered, should be wholly directed and commanded by me in everything. "Well," says I, "my conditions are but two; first, that while you stay in this island with me, you will not **pretend to**⑤ any authority here; and if I put arms in your hands, you will, upon all occasions, give them up to me, and do no **prejudice**⑥ to me or mine upon this island, and in the meantime be governed by my orders; secondly, that if the ship is or may be recovered, you will carry me and my man to England passage free."

He gave me all the assurances that the invention or faith of man could devise.

In the middle of this discourse we heard some of them awake, and soon after we saw two of them on their feet.

He took the musket I had given him in his hand, and a pistol in his belt, and his two **comrades**⑦ with him, with each man a piece in his hand; the two men who were with him going first made some noise, at

分惊讶。

“先生，”他说，“凶手近在咫尺，还是长话短说，我是那条船的船长，我手下的人背叛了我。费尽周折，凶手才答应不杀我，最后把我们3人流放到这个荒凉所在，其中一个是大副，一个是旅客。我们估计我们肯定会饿死在这里。我们确信这里没有人烟。我们正不知道如何是好呢。

“请你听着，先生，”我说，“如果我冒险救你们，你们愿意和我订两个条件吗？”他不等我把话说完，就向我说，只要把大船抢回来，他以及他的船将一切听从我的吩咐和指挥。“好吧，”我说，“我只有两个条件，第一，你们在该岛停留的时候，决不能冒犯我的权力。如果我发给你们武器，无论何时，只要我向你们收回，你们就得归还给我。你们在岛上不能反对我及我的手下人。同时，你们任何时候都得听从我的命令。第二，如果收回了那条大船，你们把我及我的手下人免费带回英国。”

他向我提出了许多保证，凡是能想到、信得过的保证，都被提出来了。

交谈之中，就见那群人中的几个似乎睡醒了，不一会儿，已经有两个人站了起来。

他手中拿着我交给他的短枪，把另一支手枪也插在皮带上。他的两个伙伴也跟着他一起过去了，每人手里拿着一杆枪。那两个跟随他走在前头的同伴大概搞出了点响动，其中一个醒来的水

① astonished /ə'staniʃt/ *a.* 惊讶的

② mutiny /'mjuːtini/ *v.* 兵变，叛变

③ desolate /'desəlit/ *a.* 荒凉的

④ anticipate /æn'tisipeit/ *v.* 预期，期待

⑤ pretend to 自称具有

⑥ prejudice /'predʒudis/ *n.* 偏见，伤害

⑦ comrade /'kɔmrid/ *n.* 同志

which one of the seamen who was awake turned about, and seeing them coming, cried out to the rest; but it was too late then, for the moment he cried out they fired—I mean the two men, the captain wisely reserving his own piece. They had so well aimed their shot at the men they knew, that one of them was killed on the spot, and the other very much wounded; but not being dead, he started up on his feet, and called eagerly for help to the other; but the captain stepping to him, told him it was too late to cry for help, he should call upon God to forgive his **villainy**①, and with that word knocked him down with the stock of his musket, so that he never spoke more.

And by and by three straggling men, that were (happily for them) parted from the rest, came back upon hearing the guns fired; and seeing the captain, who was before their prisoner, now their **conqueror**②, they **submitted**③ to be bound also; and so our victory was complete.

Upon this, it presently occurred to me that in a little while the ship's **crew**④, wondering what was become of their comrades and of the boat, would certainly come on shore in their other boat to look for them, and that then, perhaps, they might come armed, and be too strong for us.

Upon this, I told him the first thing we had to do was to **stave**⑤ the boat which lay upon the beach, so that they might not carry her off, and taking everything out of her.

While we were thus preparing our designs, and had first, by main strength, **heaved**⑥ the boat upon the beach, so high that the tide would not float her off at high-water mark, and besides, had broke a hole in her bottom too big to be quickly stopped, and were set down musing what we should do, we heard the ship fire a gun, and saw her make a

手听见了响动，转过身随即看见他们过来了，就向其余的人大声叫唤，但尚未叫出声，他们就开枪了，我指的是船长的那两个伙伴，而船长很聪明地没开枪，保留着自己的子弹。他们的枪打得很准，当场打死了一个，而且另一个受了重伤，但还没死，他摇摇晃晃地站了起来，急忙向其他人呼救。船长一步跳到他眼前，对他说现在呼救已经太晚了，他应该请求上帝宽恕他的罪行，说罢一枪把他打倒在地，叫他再也甭想开口说话。

片刻功夫，那3个到别处闲逛的人（他们真是好运气）没有跟那些人在一起，听见枪声后也回来了，一看见船长从当初的犯人一跃而为征服者，他们也就俯首就缚了，成了我们的俘虏。就这样，我们获得了全胜。

我想到再过一会儿，大船上的船员一定会奇怪他们的伙伴和小船去哪里，必然要乘大船上另一只小艇到岸上找他们，那时说不定他们会带着武器来，实力远远超过我们。

于是，我告诉船长，我们首先要把沙滩上的小船凿破，把上面所有的东西都拿下来，使它失去航行的能力，叫他们没办法开走。

然后我们就依照计划进行部署，首先是全力以赴将小船推到沙滩高处，使海水在高潮时不至于没过船的最高水位线，然后我们又在船底凿了个大洞，大得短时间内无法堵住。我们正坐在地上，琢磨下一步怎么办，只听见那艘大船放了一

① villainy /ˈviləni/ *n.* 坏事，恶行

② conqueror /ˈkɔŋkərə/ *n.* 征服者，胜利者

③ submit /səbˈmit/ *v.* 服从，屈服

④ crew /kru/*n.* 全体船员

⑤ stave /steiv/ *v.* 敲破

⑥ heave /hiːv/ *v.* 用力举起，凸起

waft with her **ensign**[1] as a signal for the boat to come on board—but no boat stirred; and they fired several times, making other signals for the boat. At last, when all their signals and firing proved fruitless, and they found the boat did not stir, we saw them, by the help of my glasses, **hoist**[2] another boat out and row towards the shore.

We had, upon the first appearance of the boat's coming from the ship, considered of separating our prisoners; and we had, indeed, secured them effectually. Two of them, of whom the captain was less assured than ordinary, I sent with Friday, and one of the three delivered men, to my cave.

The other prisoners had better usage; two of them were kept **pinioned**[3], indeed, because the captain was not able to trust them; but the other two were taken into my service, upon the captain's recommendation, and upon their solemnly engaging to live and die with us; so with them and the three honest men we were seven men, well armed; and I made no doubt we should be able to deal well enough with the ten that were coming, considering that the captain had said there were three or four honest men among them also. As soon as they got to the place where their other boat lay, they ran their boat into the beach and came all on shore, hauling the boat up after them.

Being on shore, the first thing they did, they ran all to their other boat; and it was easy to see they were under a great surprise to find her **stripped**[4], as above, of all that was in her, and a great hole in her bottom. After they had mused a while upon this, they set up two or three great shouts, hallooing with all their might, to try if they could make their companions hear; but all was to no purpose. Accordingly, they immediately launched their boat again, and got all of them on

① ensign /'ensain/ *n.* 国旗

② hoist /hɔist/ *v.* 升起，举起

③ pinion /'pinjən/ *v.* 绑住……两臂

④ strip /strip/ *v.* 剥，拆

枪，晃动旗帜，示意回去，可是他们看不见小船的动静。于是，他们接着又放了几枪，向小船又发出一些别的信号。最后，也许看到发信号和放枪毫无结果，小船也不见动静，我从望远镜里看见，他们把另外一只小艇放下来，向岸上摇过来。

自从我们看见那只小船从大船旁开过来，我们就考虑把俘虏分散开。他们这群人中有两个人让船长不放心，我派星期五和船长的一个伙伴把他们送到洞里去。

其余俘虏所受待遇相对较好。这些俘虏中只有两个始终没有松绑，因为船长不相信他们。但另外两个受到船长的推荐，而他们也发誓要和我们共患难，因而得到我的录用。所以，加上他们和船长那 3 人，我们现在已经有 7 个人，都是全副武装。我坚信我们完全能够对付那 10 个人，因为船长曾经说过，他们那些人中间也有三四个好人。那些人来到头一只小船停泊的地方，立刻把他们的小船开到沙滩上，一起上岸，然后把小船拉到了岸上。

上岸之后，他们做的第一件事就是向先前那只小船跑去。不难想像，当发现船上东西都被拿光，而船底又有一个大洞时，他们大惊失色。他们盘算了一会儿，然后，就扯着嗓子大喊了两三声，看看他们的伙伴是否能听见，可是一切全无结果。于是，他们马上把小船推到水里，一齐上了船。

board.

They had not been long put off with the boat, when we perceived them all coming on shore again; but with this new measure in their conduct, which it seems they consulted together upon, viz., to leave three men in the boat, and the rest to go on shore, and go up into the country to look for their fellows.

The seven men came on shore, and the three who remained in the boat put her off to a good distance from the shore, and came to an anchor to wait for them.

Those that came on shore kept close together, marching towards the top of the little hill under which my habitation lay.

But when they were come to the **brow**[①] of the hill, they shouted and hallooed till they were weary; and not caring, it seems, to venture far from the shore, nor far from one another, they sat down together under a tree to consider it.

After long consultation, they all started up and marched down towards the sea.

As soon as I perceived them go towards the shore, I imagined it to be as it really was that they had given over their search, and were going back again; and the captain, as soon as I told him my thoughts, was ready to sink at the apprehensions of it; but I presently thought of a **stratagem**[②] to fetch them back again, and which answered my end to a **tittle**[③]. I ordered Friday and the captain's mate to go over the little creek westward, towards the place where the savages came on shore, when Friday was rescued, and so soon as they came to a little rising round, at about half a mile distant, I bade them halloo out, as loud as they could, and wait till they found the seamen heard them; that as soon as

他们开走小船不大一会儿，我们又看见他们一齐又回到岸上，但是，他们采取了新的行动。看样子，他们刚才都商量好了，那就是留 3 个人看船，其余的人一齐上岸，到岛上的荒野中去寻找他们那些失踪的伙伴。

那 7 个人上岸以后，留在小船上的那 3 位就把船开到了离岸稍远的地方，停泊在那里，等候上岸的人。

那些登上岸的人，紧紧靠在一起，朝那个小山头前进。而我的住所，就座落在这小山底下。

可是，他们一来到山坡上就大喊大叫起来，直到他们喊得疲倦不堪。看来他们无意冒险深入远离海岸的地带，也不愿意彼此分散，接着他们在一棵大树下坐下，考虑办法。

他们商量了半天，忽然一齐跳起来，向海边走去。

我一见他们向海边走，猜测他们已经放弃了搜查，准备再次返回。我马上把自己的想法告诉船长，他一下子陷入了沉思。不过我突然想出一个吸引他们回来的法子，事实上，最终结果不出我所料。我派星期五和那位船长的大副越过小河往西走，一直走到我救星期五时野人登陆的地方，并且叫他们走到半里以外的一块地势较高的地方，一到那儿我就让他们尽量高声喊叫，以他们最大的嗓门高喊，一直喊到那些水手听见为止。又让他们在听见那些水手的答应之后，再回叫几声，然后别让他们看见，绕上一个大圈，一

① brow /brau / *n.* 山顶

② stratagem /'strætidʒəm/ *n.* 战略，计谋

③ tittle /'titl/ *n.* 些量，微量 to a tittle 精确地

ever they heard the seamen answer them, they should return it again; and then, keeping out of sight, take a round, always answering when the others hallooed, to draw them as far into the island and among the woods as possible, and then wheel about again to me by such ways as I directed them.

They were just going into the boat when Friday and the mate hallooed; and they presently heard them, and answering, ran along the shore westward, towards the voice they heard, when they were stopped by the creek, where the water being up, they could not get over, and called for the boat to come up and set them over; as, indeed, I expected.

The boat being gone a good way into the creek, and, as it were, in a harbour within the land, they took one of the three men out of her, to go along with them, and left only two in the boat, having **fastened**① her to the stump of a little tree on the shore. This was what I wished for; and immediately leaving Friday and the captain's mate to their business, I took the rest with me; and, crossing the creek out of their sight, we surprised the two men before they were aware—one of them lying on the shore, and the other being in the boat. The fellow on shore was between sleeping and waking, and going to start up; the captain, who was **foremost**②, ran in upon him, and knocked him down; and then called out to him in the boat to yield, or he was a dead man. They needed very few arguments to persuade a single man to yield, when he saw five men upon him and his comrade knocked down; besides, this was, it seems, one of the three who were not so hearty in the **mutiny**③ as the rest of the crew, and therefore was easily persuaded not only to yield, but afterwards to join very sincerely with us. In the meantime,

面叫着，一边答应，尽可能把他们往岛的深处引，往树林里引，然后再根据我指给他们的路线迂回绕到我所在的地方来。

那些人刚要上船，星期五和大副就高声喊叫起来。他们很快就听见了，于是一边答应着，一边沿海岸往西跑，朝着他们听见的声音方向跑去，直到被一条小河挡住了去路。这时河水已涨，他们没法过河，只好把那只小船叫过来渡河。这一切不出我所料。

那条小船顺着河向上走了很长的一段距离后，到达了一个类似港口可以停放的地方，他们又从船上3个人中间叫了一个和他们一块走，只留下其余两个人看船，那船被牢牢地系在一根小木桩上。这正遂我心愿。我把星期五和大副丢开，让他们继续干他们的事，自己带着其余的人，偷偷渡过小河，出其不意地向那两个人扑去。其中一人躺在岸上，其他的人则还留在船上。岸上的那一个正似睡非睡，刚要爬起来，船长抢先把他打倒在地，然后向船上另一个大喝一声，叫他赶快投降，否则就要他的命。劝单个人投降确实是不用费什么唇舌，当那个人看见自己的同伴已被打翻在地，5个人向他扑来，投降也是预料之中的事，况且看起来他是对暴动不太热心的3名水手之一。他不仅立刻投降了我们，还成为我们队伍中忠实的一员。就在这时，星期五和大副的任务完成得很出色。他们一边喊着，一边答应着，把那些人从一座小山引到另一座小

① fasten /ˈfɑːsn/ *v.* 拴紧，使固定

② foremost /ˈfɔːməust/ *a.* 在最前面

③ mutiny /ˈmjuːtini/ *n.* 兵变，反抗

Friday and the captain's mate so well managed their business with the rest that they drew them, by hallooing and answering, from one hill to another, and from one wood to another, till they not only heartily tired them, but left them where they were very sure they could not reach back to the boat before it was dark; and, indeed, they were heartily tired themselves also, by the time they came back to us.

It was several hours after Friday came back to me before they came back to their boat. At length they came up to the boat; but it is impossible to express their confusion when they found the boat fast aground in the creek, the tide ebbed out, and their two men gone.

Therefore, to make sure of them, I drew my **ambuscade**① nearer, and ordered Friday and the captain to **creep**② upon their hands and feet, as close to the ground as they could, that they might not be discovered, and get as near them as they could possibly before they offered to fire.

The **boatswain**③ was killed upon the spot; the next man was shot in the body, and fell just by him, though he did not die till an hour or two after; and the third ran for it.

We came upon them, indeed, in the dark, so that they could not see our number; and I made the man they had left in the boat, who was now one of us, to call them by name, to try if I could bring them to a **parley**④, and so perhaps might reduce them to terms; which fell out just as we desired: for indeed it was easy to think, as their condition then was, they would be very willing to **capitulate**⑤.

In a word, they all laid down their arms and begged their lives; and I sent the man that had parleyed with them, and two more, who bound them all.

山，从一片树林引到另一片树林，不但把他们搞得筋疲力竭，而且把他们引到一个很远的地方，不到天黑，绝对回不了他们的小船。不用说那些人，即使是星期五和大副，当他们回到我们中间时，也已经疲惫不堪了。

那些人一直等到星期五回来一会儿后，才绕回到他们的小船。他们总算走到小船跟前了。可是，当他们发现潮水已经退了，小船已经搁浅在小河里，而看船的两个人又不知去向时，他们那种惊慌失措的样子，不知该如何形容。

为了更有把握制服他们，我把埋伏向前推进了一段距离，命令星期五和船长尽可能贴着地面向前爬行，避免让他们发现，并且在他们动手开枪以前，爬得离他们越近越好。

那个水手头目当场被击毙，另外一个中弹倒在他身旁，过了一两个小时才死去。第三个人拔腿跑了。

我们是在黑乎乎的夜色里向他们进攻，所以他们也不知道我们有多少人。我叫那个原来留在小船上现在归降我们的那个人喊那些人的名字，看看能不能与他们谈判，强迫他们投降。结果甚合我们的心愿；不难设想在他们所处的那种境地，他们情愿投降。

总之，他们都放下了武器，请求饶命。我命令那个和他们谈判的人和其他两个把他们绑起来。

这时候我突然想到，我们得救的机会已经到

① ambuscade /ˌæmbəs'keid/ *n.* 埋伏，伏兵

② creep /kri:p/ *v.* 爬，徐行

③ boatswain /'bəutswein/ *n.* 水手长

④ parley /'pa:li/ *n.* 和谈，会谈

⑤ capitulate /kə'pitjuleit/ *v.* 有条件投降

It now occurred to me that the time of our deliverance was come, and that it would be a most easy thing to bring these fellows in to be hearty in getting possession of the ship. Upon the captain coming to me, I told him my project for seizing the ship, which he liked wonderfully well, and resolved to put it in execution the next morning.

Our strength was now thus ordered for the expedition: first, the captain, his mate, and passenger; second, the two prisoners of the first **gang**[①], to whom, having their character from the captain, I had given their liberty, and trusted them with arms; third, the other two that I had kept till now in my **bower**[②], pinioned, but on the captain's motion had now released; fourth, these five released at last; so that there were twelve in all, besides five we kept prisoners in the cave for **hostages**[③].

The captain now had no difficulty before him, but to furnish his two boats, stop the breach of one, and man them. He made his passenger captain of one, with four of the men; and himself, his mate, and five more, went in the other; and they contrived their business very well, for they came up to the ship about midnight. As soon as they came within call of the ship, he made one of the five men named Robinson hail them, and tell them they had brought off the men and the boat, but that it was a long time before they had found them, and the like, holding them in a chat till they came to the ship's side; when the captain and the mate entering first with their arms, immediately knocked down the second mate and carpenter with the butt-end of their muskets, being very faithfully seconded by their men; they secured all the rest that were upon the main and quarter decks, and began to fasten the **hatches**[④], to keep them down that were below; when the other boat and their men, entering at the **forechains**[⑤], secured the forecastle of the

了。现在要叫这帮人去夺取那条大船，并不是什么难事。船长来了之后，我就把夺船计划告诉了他。他听了之后非常赞同，决定在第二天早晨实行。

我们出征的兵力是这样布署的：

一、船长、大副、旅客；二、第一批水手中的两个俘虏，我从船长那儿了解了他们的人品，已经恢复其自由，并发给了他们武器；三、另外两个水手，曾被捆起来关在我的茅舍中，经船长建议，也把他们释放了；四、那5个最后被释放的人。因此，除关在石洞中的5个被当作人质的俘虏外，一共有12个人。

船长开始布署他的两只小船，把其中一只的窟窿补好，再把人手派上去，就没什么难事了。船长派他的旅客当了一只小船的船长，带了4个人。他自己、大副以及其余的5个人，上了另一只小船。他们进展很顺利，到了半夜，小船就已经开到了大船旁边。当他们开到能够向大船喊话的时候，船长命令一个叫小罗平的船员与他们打招呼，告诉他们，人和船花了很长时间才找了回来，一方面用这些话敷衍他们，另一方面向大船不断靠拢。靠拢大船之后，船长和大副首先带枪上了船，在他们忠心耿耿的手下人的帮助下，用枪把子打倒了二副和木匠，随后又把前后甲板上剩下的各色人等制服，把舱口关上，这样就把舱底下的人关在了下面。这时，第二条小船上的人也从船头的铁链子爬上来，把船的前部和通向普

① gang /gæŋ/ *n.* 队，群，帮

② bower /ˈbauə/ *n.* 凉亭，茅舍

③ hostage /ˈhɔstidʒ/ *n.* 人质

④ hatch /hætʃ/ *n.* 舱口

⑤ forechain /ˈfɔːtʃein/ *n.* 前索条

ship, and the **scuttle**[1] which went down into the cook-room, making three men they found there prisoners.

When the mate, with a crow, **split**[2] open the door, the new captain and his men fired boldly among them, and wounded the mate with a musket ball, which broke his arm, and wounded two more of the men, but killed nobody. The mate, calling for help, rushed, however, into the round-house, wounded as he was, and, with his pistol, shot the new captain through the head, the bullet entering at his mouth, and came out again behind one of his ears, so that he never spoke a word more: upon which the rest yielded, and the ship was taken effectually, without any more lives lost.

As soon as the ship was thus secured, the captain ordered seven guns to be fired, which was the signal agreed upon with me to give me notice of his success, which, you may be sure, I was very glad to hear, having sat watching upon the shore for it till near two o'clock in the morning.

I was at first ready to sink down with the surprise; for I saw my deliverance, indeed, visibly put into my hands, all things easy, and a large ship just ready to carry me away whither I pleased to go.

All this time the poor man was in as great an **ecstasy**[3] as I, only not under any surprise as I was; and he said a thousand kind and tender things to me, to compose and bring me to myself; but such was the flood of joy in my breast, that it put all my spirits into confusion: at last it broke out into tears, and in a little while after I recovered my speech; I then took my turn, and embraced him as my deliverer, and we rejoiced together.

We began to consult what was to be done with the prisoners we

① scuttle /ˈskʌtl/ *n.* 天窗

② split /split/ *v.* 分开，劈开

③ ecstasy /ˈekstəsi/ *n.* 狂喜

通厨房的小舱口占领了，俘虏了他们在厨房里碰到的3个人。

这时，当大副把船长室门砸开以后，新船长及其手下人不顾一切地向大副开枪，大副的胳膊被打断，另外有两个人被打伤，幸运的是没有死人。大副虽然受了伤，还是一面呼救，一面冲进船长室，朝新船长头上开了一枪，子弹打进他的嘴里，从一只耳朵后面出来，新船长就此一命呜呼。其他人见此情景，也不得不投降。大船就这样被夺回来了，再没死一个人。

把大船夺回之后，船长马上下令连放7枪，这是他和我约定好的信号，通知我事情成功了。你一定猜得出我听到这个信号十分高兴，因为我一直在岸上等候这个信号，差不多等到半夜两点钟。

起初，这个突如其来的喜讯几乎使我晕过去，因为我亲眼看见我脱险的事情要成功了，有一条大船要把我载到我愿意去的地方。

这时候，船长与我一样欣喜若狂，只是努力压抑着不像我这么冲动。他对我说了许许多多安慰的话，让我情绪稳定下来。但是，我内心这一惊一喜，几乎让我精神错乱了。我终于哭了出来。过了一会儿，我恢复了说话的能力。于是我又走过去拥抱他，把他当作救命恩人。两个人欢喜不尽。

我和船长开始商议怎样处理手中的这些俘虏，这件事的确需要详加考虑，我们要决定是否冒险带上他们一起走，特别是其中有两个家伙，在我们看来是死到临头也绝不悔改的。船长说，他知道这些坏蛋是无法给予宽容的，即使把他们带

had; for it was worth considering whether we might venture to take them with us or no, especially two of them, whom he knew to be **incorrigible**① and **refractory**② to the last degree; and the captain said he knew they were such **rogues**③ that there was no obliging them, and if he did carry them away, it must be in irons, as **malefactors**④, to be delivered over to justice at the first English colony he could come to.

Upon this, I told him that, if he desired it, I would undertake to bring the two men he spoke of to make it their own request that he should leave them upon the island. "I should be very glad of that," says the captain, "with all my heart." "Well," says I, "I will send for them up and talk with them for you."

One of them answered in the name of the rest, that they had nothing to say but this, that when they were taken the captain promised them their lives, and they humbly **implored**⑤ my mercy. But I told them I knew not what mercy to show them; for as for myself, I had resolved to **quit**⑥ the island with all my men, and had taken passage with the captain to go to England; and as for the captain, he could not carry them to England other than as prisoners in irons, to be tried for mutiny and running away with the ship; the consequence of which, they must needs know, would be the **gallows**⑦; so that I could not tell what was best for them, unless they had a mind to take their fate in the island. If they desired that, I did not care, as I had liberty to leave the island, I had some inclination to give them their lives, if they thought they could shift on shore. They seemed very thankful for it, and said they would much rather venture to stay there than be carried to England to be hanged. So I left it on that issue.

When they had all declared their willingness to stay, I then told

走，也必须把他们像犯人似的锁起来，等船开到任何一个英国殖民地，就把他们送交法办。

我对船长说，如果他愿意，我可以负责说服他提到过的那两个人主动请求留在岛上。船长说："如果能这样的话，我真是太高兴了，我正求之不得这样做呢。""好吧，"我说，"我现在就把他们叫来，替你跟他们谈谈。"

这时，这些俘虏当中有一个人代表他们说，他们无话可说，只是他们投降的时候，船长曾答应他们活命，他们现在只有低头恳求我的宽恕。可是我告诉他们，我不知道自己该怎样宽恕他们，因为就我而言，我已经决定带着我所有的人离开岛屿，跟船长一起搭船动身回英国。至于船长，除了把他们当作囚犯锁起来，以谋反罪的罪名送交当局法办以外，船长是不愿意把他们带回英国的。这样做的结果，他们也应该知道，一定是上绞刑架。因此，我确实替他们想不出更好的办法来，除非他们留在岛上，碰碰运气。如果他们同意这个意见，我不反对，因为我反正是要离开这个岛屿的。如果他们肯在岛上自谋出路，我愿意饶他们不死。他们对这个办法表示感激，说他们宁可冒险留在这里，也不愿被带回英国绞死。我同意他们这样做。

当他们一致表示愿意留在岛上时，我告诉他们，我要把我在岛上的生活情形讲给他们听，教导他们怎样过好生活。

我又把不久要来岛上的16位西班牙人的事情

① incorrigible /in'kɔridʒəbl/ *a.* 无药可救的，积习难改的

② refractory /ri'fræktəri/ *a.* 不听话的，执拗的

③ rogue /rəug/ *n.* 流氓

④ malefactor /'mælifæktə/ *n.* 罪人，犯人

⑤ implore /im'plɔ/ *v.* 恳求，哀求

⑥ quit /kwit/ *v.* 离开

⑦ gallows/'gæləuz/ *n.* 绞刑架

them I would let them into the story of my living there, and put them into the way of making it easy to them.

I told them the story also of the sixteen Spaniards that were to be expected, for whom I left a letter, and made them promise to treat them in common with themselves.

I left them my firearms—viz. five muskets, three fowling-pieces, and three swords. I had above a barrel and a half of powder left; for after the first year or two I used but little, and wasted none. I gave them a description of the way I managed the goats, and directions to milk and fatten them, and to make both butter and cheese. In a word, I gave them every part of my own story; and told them I should prevail with the captain to leave them two barrels of gunpowder more, and some garden-seeds, which I told them I would have been very glad of.

Having done all this I left them the next day, and went on board the ship. We prepared immediately to sail, but did not **weigh**[①] that night. The next morning early, two of the five men came swimming to the ship's side, and making the most lamentable complaint of the other three, begged to be taken into the ship for God's sake, for they should be murdered, and begged the captain to take them on board, though he hanged them immediately.

And thus I left the island, the 19th of December, as I found by the ship's account, in the year 1686, after I had been upon it eight-and-twenty years, two months, and nineteen days; being delivered from this second **captivity**[②] the same day of the month that I first made my escape in the long-boat from among the Moors of Sallee. In this vessel, after a long voyage, I arrived in England the 11th of June, in the year 1687, having been thirty-five years absent.

告诉了他们。我给那些西班牙人写了一封信，让他们彼此平等相待。

我的枪械都留给了他们，这包括有 5 支火枪，3 支鸟枪，3 把刀剑。我还留下一桶半火药，这些我过去用得很节省，一点都没浪费。我把自己养羊的办法告诉了他们。另外还把挤羊奶和如何把羊养肥、怎样挤奶、怎样做黄油和干酪的方法告诉了他们。总之，我把我自己的故事原原本本讲给他们听，还对他们说，我会劝船长再给他们留下两桶火药和一些菜种，我告诉他们，我非常愿意这样做。

办完这些事以后，我第二天就上了船，把他们留在那里。我们立即为航海做准备，但当晚并未出海。第二天一大早，留守在岛屿的那 5 个人中，有两个人泅水到船边，苦苦哀求我们看在上帝的份上准许他们上船，不然的话，那 3 个人现在歧视他们，将来准会把他们害死。他们请求船长收留他们，哪怕立刻把他们吊死，他们也心甘情愿。

就这样我离开这座小岛，我翻看一下船上的记录，我知道那天是 1686 年 12 月 19 日，我在这个海岛共居住了 28 年两个月零 19 天。我这次逃难的日期，恰好与我从摩尔人手里逃出的那天同月同日。我乘坐的这条船经过长途跋涉，终于在 1687 年 6 月 11 日抵达英国。我离开英国已 35 年了。

① weigh/wei/ *v.* 起锚

② captivity /kæp'tiviti/ *n.* 囚禁

www.ingramcontent.com/pod-product-compliance
Ingram Content Group UK Ltd.
Pitfield, Milton Keynes, MK11 3LW, UK
UKHW062003290726
14090UKWH00022B/1369